THE FORENSIC
RECORDS SOCIETY

MAGNUS MILLS

ISIS
LARGE
PRINT

First published in Great Britain 2017
by
Bloomsbury Publishing
an imprint of Bloomsbury Publishing Plc

First Isis Edition
published 2018
by arrangement with
Bloomsbury Publishing Plc

A catalogue record for this book is available
from the British Library.

ISBN 978–1–78541–533–3 (hb)
ISBN 978–1–78541–539–5 (pb)

Published by
F. A. Thorpe (Publishing)
Anstey, Leicestershire

Set by Words & Graphics Ltd.
Anstey, Leicestershire
Printed and bound in Great Britain by
T. J. International Ltd., Padstow, Cornwall

This book is printed on acid-free paper

For Sue

THE FORENSIC RECORDS SOCIETY

Two men with a passion for vinyl found a society for the appreciation of records. Their aim is simple: to elevate the art of listening by doing so in forensic detail. The society enjoys moderate success in the back room of their local pub, the Half Moon, with other enthusiasts drawn to the initial promise of the weekly gathering. However, as the club gains popularity, its founders' uncompromising dogma results in a schism within the movement, and soon a counter-group forms. Then the introduction of a young woman called Alice further fractures the unity of the vulnerable society . . .

"I saw you!"

We listened closely. The voice sounded slightly remote, as if it came from an adjoining room. It was followed by a fuzzy silence.

James gazed at the turntable as it ground to a halt.

"That's Keith," he said.

"You certain?" I asked.

"Yes."

"Not Roger?"

"No."

He played the record through for the third time. This was the agreed number of plays, so he then removed it from the turntable and returned it to its sleeve. As he did so he gave the label a cursory glance.

"Fabulous music," he remarked.

I rose from my seat and went over to the window. Outside there was snow lying everywhere.

"Do you realise," I said, "we were probably the only people on the planet listening to that?"

"Surely not," replied James.

"Just think about it," I continued. "They released it almost fifty years ago and it was a moderate success before disappearing without a trace. You never hear it on the radio these days, or anywhere else for that matter. The song was a deliberate joke: the lyrics are childish to say the least. They're practically meaningless in English, let alone Chinese, French or Russian."

"Marvellous ensemble performance nonetheless," said James.

"Of course."

I stood gazing through the glass. At any moment I expected to hear another record begin playing, but instead there was nothing. The room had fallen unusually quiet. A minute went by before finally I turned from the window and saw that James was deep in thought. He stared blankly at the Schweppes boxes and the laden shelves as if pondering some question of infinite importance.

"What about the other pressing?" he asked at length.

"Different ending," I said. "Doesn't count."

"No, I suppose not."

"Besides," I added, "nobody else is interested. Nobody listens. Not properly anyway. Not like we do."

James leaned back on the table. He had gone rather pale and was clearly shocked by my words.

"It's beyond comprehension," he murmured. "Think of all the people in all the towns and cities in the world: I can't believe there isn't somebody playing it somewhere."

I shook my head slowly.

"Sorry," I said. "I can assure you that we're quite alone."

Outside the window the sky was darkening. There was more snow on the way and it would soon be time

2

to leave. However, in view of my recent revelation I was reluctant to abandon James just yet, so when he suggested making a pot of tea I agreed to stay a while longer.

"Anyway," he said, "we've got to solve this problem before you go."

We adjourned to the kitchen and he put the kettle on; then the discussion resumed. It seemed that my chance observation had alerted James to a situation he'd never previously recognised, and now he was determined to do something about it.

"I think it's worth one last try," he said. "A final attempt to make contact with others who are like-minded."

I gave a shrug.

"What do you propose," I said, "exactly?"

"Well," said James, "there's an idea I've been nurturing for a long time but never brought to fruition."

"Oh yes?"

"We could form a society for the express purpose of listening to records closely and in detail, forensically if you like, without any interruption or distraction. There would be regular gatherings, and membership would depend on some kind of test to make sure people are genuinely interested."

"You mean a code of conduct?"

"Certainly," said James. "We don't want any charlatans."

He stirred the tea while I considered his idea.

"Where will we hold these meetings?" I enquired. "Up the pub?"

"Good thinking," James replied. "Actually I hadn't planned that far ahead, but now you come to mention it they've got a back room they don't use, haven't they? We could borrow that."

James had a sparkle in his eyes which he usually reserved for only his best records, and I had to admit the feeling was infectious. Was it really possible, I wondered, to connect with others like ourselves? There was only one way to find out, so we agreed to meet the same evening in the Half Moon.

Prior to leaving home I flipped slowly through the whole of my record collection, searching for nothing in particular, but simply absorbing the endless assortment of labels, performers and song titles. I thought this would be a good preparation for my appointment with James. I'd left him working at his kitchen table with a pencil and paper, drawing up a list of possible formats for the proposed society. The project had evidently seized his imagination, and I was eager to lend as much support as I could. An over-arching grasp of the subject was therefore indispensable. At the same time I remained convinced that my original theory was correct: there were some records that were never heard on planet Earth unless I (or James) happened to be playing them.

I completed my casual trawl of the boxes from A to Z before making a random selection: a black-and-white sleeve and a black label bearing the words PRODUCED BY BRIAN & MURRY WILSON. The sight of it made me smile to myself. This was a perfect example: not a rarity in the sense of scarceness (it probably sold a million copies in its day) but nevertheless a record that had largely been forgotten. The odds against somebody playing it at any particular moment were immeasurable. With this sobering thought in mind I returned it to its box.

Outside, the night sky was heavy with impending snow. I put my coat on and headed for the Half Moon, arriving at nine o'clock precisely. James was already there, sitting at the counter with a pint of Guinness.

"There's one for you in the pump," he announced.

George was occupied behind the bar, but when he noticed me he gave me a nod and began filling a glass.

"Have you asked him yet?" I enquired.

"No," said James. "I thought I'd wait until it was a bit quieter."

The place was fairly busy. In consequence it wasn't until almost ten that we managed to have a word with George. He worked hard during the intervening hour, but he must have detected a conspiratorial air between James and me because he kept glancing in our direction. Finally, during a brief hiatus, he came over and spoke to us.

"What are you two scheming about?" he demanded.

"Well," said James, "we were wondering if the back room would be available on Monday evenings?"

"Might be," said George. "Depends what for."

"We were thinking of starting a forensic records society."

"Oh yes?" George leaned in closer and lowered his voice. "Police work, is it?"

"Of course not," I said. "We mean records to listen to."

"Music?"

"Yes."

"There's a dartboard in the corner," said George. "Isn't that enough entertainment?"

"It's not quite the same," I replied.

"Or you may like to try a game of chess."

James ignored this distraction and stuck doggedly to his brief.

"Doesn't have to be Mondays," he said, "but we thought it might help improve trade on a quiet night."

"Oh, did you now?" said George.

Despite his bluff response, I could tell he was faintly intrigued by the proposition, especially when he realised he might sell more beer. By the time James had outlined exactly what he envisaged he'd won the publican over. He told us we could have the back room free-of-charge for a trial period of three months. There was only one proviso:

"You won't play them too loud, will you?"

"Definitely not," affirmed James. "It'll be connoisseurs only. We're not interested in excessive volume."

It was tempting to qualify this last statement (the question of loudness was entirely relative) but in the event I decided to let it go. After all, there was little point in upsetting the apple-cart at this early stage. Having reached agreement, James delved into his inside pocket and produced a large sheet of paper, folded in four.

"I've prepared an advertisement," he disclosed, opening up the document and laying it on the counter. The notice was hand-drawn in red and black felt tip:

FORENSIC RECORDS SOCIETY
MEETS HERE
MONDAYS 9PM
ALL WELCOME: BRING THREE RECORDS OF
YOUR CHOICE

Apparently James had taken it upon himself to decide the formula. I was slightly surprised that he hadn't bothered to consult with me, especially as it was supposed to be a joint project. On the other hand, I had to admit he'd devised an impressive blueprint.

"I thought three goes per person would provide a nice balance," he explained. "Not too many and not too few. Records would be played in strict rotation, of course, which should ensure a degree of variety. Obviously there will be no comments or judgement of other people's tastes. We'll be here simply to listen."

"Forensically," said George.

"Correct."

I thought I saw a rather sad expression cross George's face when he turned away, as if he'd just heard some unfortunate news. I had no notion what might have caused this, but I made a mental note to be careful in future to treat him with kindness and sympathy.

Meanwhile, James went and pinned the notice on the wall.

"By the way," I said, when he came back, "what are we going to play them on?"

"I've already thought of that," he answered. "I'll bring along my red portable."

James was the owner of three portable record players (including a model that was powered solely by batteries); he also possessed a 4-speed auto-stacker and a conventional deck with a forty-watt amplifier and twin speakers. I'd never known him take any of this equipment beyond the sanctuary of his own home, and again I was impressed by his dedication to the fledgling society. I only hoped that he wasn't going to be disappointed. I'd seen a couple of people idly watching him while he pinned up his notice, but as yet nobody had actually gone over to see what it said. Still, there was plenty of time yet: today was only Thursday.

"Will you require any sandwiches?" asked George, when we departed the pub at half past eleven.

"Probably not for the first meeting," said James, "but we'll have a look at the attendance and let you know."

I was pleased to note that James retained some degree of realism.

Outside it was snowing. We said goodnight and went our separate ways, and as I wandered home I began to consider the options that lay ahead. It struck me that I seldom had the opportunity to impose my choice of music upon other people (except James), especially under such exacting conditions. James had specified that there would be no "comments or judgement" but, even so, the clinical format made close scrutiny inescapable. Presumably this was why he insisted on using the term "forensic". (He later informed me it derived from the Latin *forensis*: "in open court".) I knew from experience that James was an impartial listener who always kept his own counsel. Indeed, I'd witnessed him sit through the entire length of records which he thoroughly loathed without showing the slightest emotion. Such generosity was rarely reciprocated, of course, and I wondered what we were letting ourselves in for. James and I would certainly adhere to the rules, but could we enforce them on others? Only time would tell. In the meantime I realised I was going to have to be careful when I made my selection.

The next few days dragged by slowly, but at last Monday evening rolled into view. I arrived at the Half Moon early (eight o'clock) and headed directly for the back room to help James with his preparations. I discovered him trying to manhandle a large round table towards the centre of the floor.

"Grab hold of this, will you?" he said, by way of greeting.

The two of us moved the table into position underneath a light bulb, then we began placing chairs around it. It was the first time I'd been in this room and as I glanced about I noticed a small, unused bar in the corner, complete with three beer pumps.

"I didn't know they served drinks in here," I remarked.

"They don't," said James. "Haven't for years."

A number of tables and chairs were stacked in the other corners, and the room had a definite "forgotten" feel about it. Still, the sight of James's red portable was most cheering. He'd had the forethought of bringing

9

along an extension cable too, and once he'd plugged in we were all set to go.

"What's the time?" he asked.

"Five past eight."

"Is that all?"

"Yep."

"Right," he announced, "we'll get a couple of pints and await our guests."

"Oh," I said. "You don't think we should have a trial run then?"

James stood regarding me with a look of mild astonishment on his face, as though he couldn't believe what he'd just heard.

"Absolutely not," he said. "The purpose of these meetings is to raise the art of listening to a higher level. That's why we booked this room in the first place: otherwise we might as well go and listen to a jukebox in some crowded dive. The whole idea is to play records under controlled conditions according to a strict timetable. A trial run would completely dispel the sense of occasion we're hoping to engender."

At that moment a bearded man stuck his head round the door, with a pint of beer in one hand and a flat, square package in the other.

"Not too late am I?" he asked.

"No, as a matter of fact you're early," James replied. "Starts at nine." His tone of voice was not quite imperious, but it was not far off it either.

"Sorry," said the man, withdrawing swiftly.

"Steady, James," I said. "We don't want to drive them all away before we start."

James said nothing and busied himself tidying up the chairs (which were already tidy). Meanwhile I went out to get some drinks. The bearded man had taken up position beside the bar, so I acknowledged him with a nod before ordering two pints of Guinness. The clock now said eight fifteen and it seemed rather unfair to leave him out here on his own for three-quarters of an hour. Nonetheless I had no desire to overrule James. This was our inaugural evening and the society wouldn't exist officially until nine o'clock. Until then the newcomer would simply have to wait. I glanced around the pub in search of other potential candidates but there were none to be seen; therefore he faced a lonely vigil. After paying for the beers I gave him a second nod and returned to the back room.

"Many out there?" James enquired.

"No," I said, "just that bloke who looked in."

"Ah well, we've got plenty of time yet."

My place at the table was indicated by three records lying in a neat little stack. I sat down and began reading the labels on both sides. James had a similar stack, and I was tempted to ask him what he'd brought along. In view of his earlier remarks, however, I sensed this would be considered inappropriate. Until the appointed hour, then, all was to remain under wraps.

At five to nine we'd almost finished our pints, so James went out to buy another round. When he returned he had the bearded man in tow. His name was Chris and despite being kept waiting in the wings his enthusiasm was undaunted.

11

"This is great," he said. "Just what I've been searching for."

Nobody else had turned up, apparently, and at the stroke of nine James went and closed the door.

"Latecomers will not be admitted," he said. "Now, Chris, would you like to get us started?"

Looking a little abashed, Chris handed over his first choice. James peered closely at the pink label but passed no comment. He placed the record on the turntable, turned the volume halfway, and we spent the next two and a half minutes listening to "The Universal".

While it was playing both James and Chris stared solemnly at the revolving disc. Neither showed any reaction to the barking dog which accompanied the opening bars, the sudden appearance of electric guitars in the middle section, nor the jokey trombone at the end. They just sat listening in reverential awe. The red portable was equipped with an automatic stop switch, and when finally it clicked off nobody spoke for several long moments. Finally Chris broke the silence:

" 'That's the sea in the trees in the morning.' "

It was all he said, but we knew exactly what he meant.

My turn came next, so I handed over a copy of "Promised Land" and James did the honours. Again he and Chris sat solemnly at the table as the record played, and again there was a long silence afterwards, broken this time by a soft knock on the door.

"Oh, who's this?" said James. "It can't be too loud: we've only got the volume halfway."

I went to the door, opened it by the merest inch and looked out. There was a short unlit passageway between the back room and the main part of the pub, and standing in the gloom was a man in a long, leather coat. It was purple in colour (or possibly maroon) with matching buttons and gigantic lapels. The man was clutching a small square box.

"Is this the Forensic Records Society?" he enquired.

"Yes," I replied, "but we've already started."

"Well, sorry for being late," he said, "but I've only just seen the notice. I rushed straight home to collect my records."

"Oh right," I said. "Just a minute then."

I closed the door and went over to James and Chris.

"There's a guy outside," I explained. "Says he had to go home and fetch his records."

"That's no excuse," said James. "We can't admit latecomers: it's too disruptive."

"Couldn't we make an exception just this once?"

"I'm afraid not."

"So what shall I say?"

"Tell him to come back next week," James answered. "It'll be a good test of his commitment."

At these words I saw Chris raise his eyebrows. He voiced no opinion, however, so I returned to the door. When I opened it the man outside peered at me expectantly. He was plainly eager to join us and I regretted having to disappoint him. I slipped into the passageway and closed the door behind me.

"Sorry," I said, adopting a conciliatory tone. "Could you come back next week?"

The eager expression faded.

"But I collected my records especially," said the man.

"Sorry," I repeated. As the moments ticked by it struck me that James should have been out here dealing with this. After all, he was the hardliner, not me. I was only the messenger. Eventually I heard the man take a deep breath; then came a final plea.

"So I can't persuade you to change your mind?"

"No."

"Very well!" he snapped, glaring at me before turning away and marching down the passage. He shoved open the outer door and next instant he was gone.

When I went back inside, James and Chris were waiting patiently.

"All dealt with?" asked Chris.

"More or less," I answered, "but he appears to have taken it quite personally."

"Never mind," said James. "He'll be alright."

I wasn't so sure, and as the meeting resumed I wondered how I'd have felt if I'd been rejected in such an abrupt manner. Actually it took me a good while to recover from the incident. In consequence I paid scant attention when James played the next record. He'd chosen "Atlantis" as his first selection, but the unfolding narrative just went right over my head. All I could picture was the look of dismay on the man's face when I told him he couldn't come in. Surely, I thought, the purpose of the society was to encourage people to embrace the cause, not deter them. This was rather different from James's definition, which verged on puritanical.

"Atlantis" was still on the wane when at last I emerged from these disquieting thoughts. Chris was gazing serenely at the red portable, while James retained his more solemn expression. All indications showed that we'd settled on a perfect formula, and therefore I decided for the time being to keep any misgivings to myself.

We each had two records remaining, and the rest of the evening went by pleasantly enough. There was unspoken agreement that our combined choices were rounded, wide-ranging and tasteful. Furthermore, Chris made it clear that he fully intended to come back the following week.

"It's great," he said. "Just what I've been searching for."

"Shame about the low turnout," remarked James, after he'd gone. "Probably due to all that snow."

I didn't bother to mention that there'd been a thaw over the weekend. The snow was long departed. We wandered out to the bar, only to discover that George was on the point of closing.

"You cut that a bit fine," he said, mercifully reaching for two fresh glasses. "You should learn to keep your eyes on the clock."

It was two minutes past eleven, and we were at a loss to explain the situation.

"We've only played nine records," I said. "Even at a stretch it should have taken an hour at the most."

"Yes, very peculiar," agreed James. "We lost a few minutes while that guy was at the door, but even so there's another hour entirely unaccounted for."

"Perhaps you were whisked away in a time machine," suggested George.

"Yes, perhaps," said James, "but whatever the reason, we'll need to be careful when membership starts building up."

"You're confident it will then, are you?" I asked.

"Of course," James replied. "Actually I originally considered a much wider advertising campaign, but on second thoughts I concluded that an organic approach would be better."

"You mean word of mouth?"

"Correct."

Apart from the two of us, the pub was now empty. George had begun polishing glasses and placing them upside down on a shelf.

"So," he said, "what's so special about these vintage records then?"

"They're not necessarily vintage," said James.

"Well, the ones you played tonight certainly were," George retorted. "I could hear them through the door and I remembered all of them from my youth."

"Those were just what we chose for this evening," explained James. "We'll have new ones as well sometimes."

"But I didn't think they made them any more."

"Certainly they do," said James. "Oh, I admit they're not as widely available as they used to be, but you can still get them if you know where to go. Even one of the flagship stores still sells them."

"Really?"

"In fact, some performers insist on including a proportion of proper records in their output."

All this was evidently news to George, and in a way I felt rather sorry for him. It was obvious he needed to get out and about a bit more. Even so, the point he'd made about us playing vintage records was quite valid: none of this evening's choices had been less than thirty years old. James could protest all he liked, but the truth was that we tended to favour the tried and tested recordings over the recent upstarts. With this in mind, I determined to bring some of my more modern acquisitions to next week's meeting.

Meanwhile, there remained the question of what to do with the red portable. James was reluctant to lug it to and fro each week, so eventually George agreed to lock it safely in the back room.

"Nobody else uses it," he said. "Only you."

It was time to leave.

"Odd about that lost hour," I said, when we got outside.

"Yes," said James. "Very odd."

I pondered the subject on my way home, but I could come up with no reasonable explanation.

I met James in the Half Moon the following Thursday. Apparently, during our absence there'd been several enquiries about the Forensic Records Society. Somebody had even demanded to know our names.

"Did you tell them?" James asked.

"Of course," said George. "They're not secret, are they?"

"No, no," said James. "Just wondered, that's all."

"Can you remember who it was?" I asked.

"Well, I was quite busy," replied George, "and I didn't pay much attention. I suppose it could have been the chap who wears the long, leather coat, but I can't really remember."

There were a few other people waiting to be served, so James and I found a table in the corner and sat down. We had a clear view of the back-room door, and after a while we saw a man with spiky hair go over and read our notice. He then went to the bar and spoke to George, who nodded in our direction. Next moment the man was standing over us.

"The perfect pop song is precisely three minutes in length," he announced. "Do you agree?"

"It depends," I said. "Would you like to sit down and discuss it?"

"Thank you."

It soon transpired that the spiky haircut matched the newcomer's personality exactly. He appeared to think that a conversation comprised a series of questions and answers fired back and forth like some frantic game of ping-pong. Moreover, he was seemingly fixated by the duration of records as expressed in minutes and seconds.

"Mike," he said by way of introduction, harshly scraping a chair into position. "'God Save the Queen'. How long?"

"Not sure," I replied. "Three minutes?"

"Three twenty," he snapped back. "'Smash It Up'. How long?"

"Don't know."

"Two fifty. 'Stand Down Margaret'. How long?"

"You tell me."

"Three thirty-two. 'Complete Control'. How long?"

"Three ten," said James.

"Oh . . . er . . . yes."

James's sudden interjection briefly knocked the wind out of Mike's sails. Or perhaps he'd simply run out of energy. Either way, his response to this evidently correct answer was to cease his cross-examination and fall silent. He sat back in his chair and stared at the pint glass he'd brought with him.

I glanced around the interior of the Half Moon. It was a usual Thursday evening and people were surging back and forth between the various local pubs. Every week was the same. They reminded me of herds of wildebeest constantly roaming from one source of water to another, never settling anywhere, and always on the move. Judging from his exuberant manner, I fully expected Mike to join the restless throng at any moment and follow them into the night. Instead, however, he seemed content to remain sitting at our table, which was a haven of stillness. The comparative quiet allowed him a few moments of reflection, and very soon he returned to his previous theme.

"Three minutes precisely," he said. "That's the objective."

He spoke as if he were uttering an immutable truth which had been handed down by some higher authority. I had no particular view on the matter and hence felt unable to contradict him, but I thought I sensed James stirring in the chair opposite mine.

"Never been attained though," Mike added.

This last assertion was too much for James. "Are you sure?" he demanded.

"Yep," came the reply. "There've been many attempts, but perfection continues to elude us."

James considered the pronouncement.

"'Hands Off . . . She's Mine'", he said. "That must be close."

"Close," said Mike, "but not close enough. Three minutes and one second."

This time it was James who fell silent. We had reached an impasse, so I took the opportunity to get another round of drinks.

"Like a pint?" I asked, peering at Mike.

"Thank you," he replied. "Lager please."

"Righto."

While I was waiting at the bar I looked back once or twice to our table in the corner. I could see Mike and James sitting side by side, both of them gazing wordlessly into space. From what I could judge, they shared obsessions that were similar but not identical, a situation which made communion between them unworkable for the present. Instead, there was an uneasy truce. Furthermore, I suspected that James disagreed with Mike's definition of perfection. I managed to obtain a tray from George, loaded it with three glasses, then quickly returned to my companions.

"This Forensic Society of yours," said Mike, as I sat down. "Open to all comers, is it?"

"Of course," I replied. "Just turn up at nine o'clock on Monday with three records of your choice."

"Any length," added James.

I thought his remark was a quite unnecessary provocation, but in the event Mike took it at face value.

"So less than three minutes is OK?"

"Certainly," I said. "Whatever you like."

"Less than two minutes?"

"Well . . ."

Before I could answer, James broke in again.

"'Like a Rolling Stone'", he said. "Six minutes precisely. Does that make it doubly perfect?"

Mike looked at James with bewilderment.

"Don't know," he said. "Never heard of it."

He downed his pint, thanked me for my generosity, then rose from the table and walked away.

"See you Monday?" I enquired.

"Yeah," he said, over his shoulder. "See you Monday."

Once Mike was lost from view, James gave a sigh.

"How could he have gone through life without ever hearing it?" he said. "Hardly seems credible."

"Maybe he was born too late," I suggested.

"Yes, maybe."

"Or perhaps his line of descent was different from ours."

"Yes."

"We'll just have to make allowances for him, that's all."

The encounter with Mike was the closest we ever got to a recruitment drive. Mostly we relied on our "organic" approach, and when I turned up the following Monday I could tell it was beginning to work.

I walked into the Half Moon and saw Chris standing at one end of the bar, and Mike at the other. There were also a couple of blokes sitting at the corner table who were obviously waiting for something to happen. As I came in, they all peered hopefully in my direction. I hadn't bothered arriving early because I knew there was no need, but according to George the rest of them (including Chris) had been there since eight o'clock.

"Where's James?" I asked. "Out the back?"

"Yes," replied George. "He's been here since eight as well."

It was five to nine, so I decided to go through to the back room to see if James was ready. To my surprise I found the door locked from the inside. I gave it a knock.

"James," I called, "it's me," and after a short delay he opened up.

"Sorry," he explained. "I had to lock it. They've all been pestering me for the past hour."

"Well," I replied, "I must say they look very eager."

"Anyway, they can come in now, if you'd like to tell them."

I obeyed his instruction and at nine o'clock we all filed into the back room. James had prepared it exactly the same as the previous week, with the red portable again taking centre stage on the table. The two newcomers, I noticed, glanced at it in a deferential manner as they drew near. They were called Dave and Barry, and each carried a small clutch of records. So did Chris, Mike and I.

"Thanks for coming everybody," said James. "Now, Barry, would you like to get proceedings underway?"

Barry handed over his first record and James laid it carefully on the turntable before switching on. The moment it started I knew what it was. Apparently, Mike did too.

" 'How I Wrote Plastic Man' ", he announced. "Four minutes nineteen seconds."

James immediately stopped the record.

"Sorry, Mike," he said, "but you must try and remember this is primarily a listening society. We don't allow comments or judgements, especially while records are playing."

"Oh, right," said Mike. "Sorry."

"Has everyone else got the message?" James added.

There was a murmur of assent.

"Good."

James was about to re-start the record when Barry spoke.

"By the way," he said. "It's 'Elastic Man'."

"Well, it sounds like 'Plastic Man' to me," said Mike.

"That's deliberate," said Dave. "He sings 'Plastic Man' to be controversial, but it's actually 'Elastic Man'."

"What's it say on the label?"

" 'Elastic Man'."

"Can we please proceed!" snapped James.

"Sorry," they all chorused, and at last he managed to play the record in its entirety. Next in turn was Mike. As I expected, he'd brought along a set of short, hard-core performances including a breakneck version of "She's Not There" which lasted barely two minutes.

My first offering was "Nothing to Fear", followed later by "Geraldine" and "That's Entertainment". Chris, on the other hand, had opted for something much more traditional. We sat around the table in our various attitudes (serene, solemn, mesmerised and so forth) and listened to the jangling introduction, a chorus, two verses, another chorus and a jangling fade-out. Afterwards there was a long silence, finally broken by Chris:

" 'Take me for a trip upon your magic, swirling ship.' "

It was all he said, but we knew exactly what he meant. Well, most of us did anyway.

"How come he's allowed to speak and not me?" demanded Mike.

"Nobody's allowed to speak," said James firmly; then, realising he'd probably overstepped the mark, he softened his tone a little. "Is there anything you'd like to add?"

"It's just that I've never heard that one before."

"You must have."

"I haven't," said Mike. "How long is it?"

James peered at the label.

"Two minutes eighteen seconds."

"Their follow-ups were even shorter," said Dave. "Two minutes two seconds and two minutes four if I'm not mistaken."

"Really?" said Mike, evidently fascinated by this information. "I'll have to check them out."

James, meanwhile, had lapsed into a resigned silence. I could see he was suffering deep inner turmoil, so I decided to intercede.

"Time for the next choice," I said.

It was Dave's turn, and he presented James with a copy of "Come As You Are". This served to revive James's interest and from then on the meeting went fairly smoothly. The only interruption came at the end of the final record, when George knocked at the door and looked in.

"You know it's almost eleven?" he said. "If you want last drinks you'd better hurry up."

We swiftly packed away our gear and headed for the bar.

"How on earth did that happen?" said James, after we'd got our pints. "We played eighteen records, so that should have been ninety minutes maximum. Even with the delays I thought we had at least another half-hour to spare."

"So did I," I said. "It's a good job George came and told us."

"Yes."

"Still a mystery, though."

After conferring with George we decided that the best solution was to bring future gatherings forward to eight o'clock.

"Can you inform the others?" said James. "I'll have to see about altering the notice."

Once we'd resolved the issue, a secondary thought occurred to me.

"I'm surprised that bloke in the long, leather coat never turned up," I said. "He seemed quite keen."

"Well," James replied, "I told you it would be a test of his commitment."

"Maybe he'll come next week."

"Yes, maybe."

We were about to leave the pub when Mike approached us, apparently seeking reassurance. He had a very earnest expression on his face.

"My records were alright, were they?" he asked.

"They were fine," I answered. "An interesting selection."

"Not too short?"

"Of course not."

"Nobody said anything."

"They wouldn't," attested James. "Comments and judgements aren't allowed."

Mike hesitated a few seconds before speaking again.

"So how do I know if they're any good?"

Now his expression was deadly serious. It was almost as if he feared being arrested by some dark agency over his choice of music. Obviously the spiky exterior masked a brittle shell.

"Doesn't really matter," said James. "As long as you like it, you can play whatever you like."

I had to admit I was rather impressed by James's response to these enquiries. Very impressed indeed. Lately I'd become concerned about his increasing intolerance during meetings of the Forensic Records Society. The way he enforced the rules verged on the despotic, yet here he was trying patiently to allay Mike's doubts and worries. In that instant I realised James was a true believer. His message was clear: people could listen to anything they chose, provided they listened properly.

Tonight, however, it was George's turn to be intolerant.

"Come on you lot!" he barked. "Out!"

We all said goodbye and went our separate ways.

Towards the end of the week I received an item of mail in the post. Inside the envelope was a leaflet:

CONFESSIONAL RECORDS SOCIETY
MEETS EVERY TUESDAY
9PM
HALF MOON
BRING A RECORD OF YOUR CHOICE AND CONFESS!

As I read the words I felt a cold chill running through me. This threatened to undermine all that James and I had achieved, and I wondered who could have been behind it. There was no covering letter or return address; nor did I recognise the handwriting on the envelope. Yet the term "confessional" sounded vaguely familiar, and I spent a while sifting through my memory trying to locate it. Eventually, though, I gave up and went round to see James instead. It transpired that he'd received an identical leaflet.

"Nothing to be concerned about," he remarked. "Plainly a total fraud."

"You mean it's a joke?" I enquired.

"Oh no," he said. "I think they're quite sincere, but these meetings are run by deluded individuals who attract similarly deluded newcomers."

James went on to explain that "confessional" gatherings originated in the United States, where they were fairly widespread. People sat in groups playing records, then each participant revealed to the others why they chose them. It seemed the events were often highly charged emotional affairs.

"But they don't listen properly," James concluded. "It's all a fake."

Even so, the Confessional Records Society had now arrived on our doorstep, a development which I for one found most unsettling. Furthermore, it could hardly have been a coincidence that the first meeting was scheduled to take place in the Half Moon.

"Yes, it is rather close to home," said James. "Fortunately it's fixed for Tuesday, so it shouldn't impinge on us."

"Won't it affect our membership?" I asked.

"Probably not," he replied. "This 'confessionalism' appeals to a different kind of person altogether."

"Yes, I suppose you're right," I said. "I can't imagine having to explain some of my choices: 'Leggo Skanga', for example, or 'Cockney Translation'."

"They're beyond words," said James.

"Precisely."

He told me he was just about to put the kettle on, so we went through to the kitchen and sat down at the table.

"Been busy?" I ventured.

"Yes, I have actually," he said. "I've been engaged all morning on a side-project of mine."

"Oh yes?"

"About a month ago I decided to play my entire collection in strict alphabetical order. Obviously I can only do it when I've got a moment to spare. I've just started working my way through the D's."

"Still a long way to go then?"

"Yes, there's about nine hundred all told."

James added that this was a valuable pastime because he could combine research with recreation. He'd already picked out several suitable contenders for our next visit to the Half Moon. James planned to continue his side-project during the afternoon, and I ended up "sitting in" on the session for several hours. It was a gruelling process because a few of his "E" records had begun to sound rather dated (we both agreed about that), but we pressed on all the same and I think he was thankful for my support. By the time I departed, we'd made good progress into the F's.

"Don't forget," he said, "we meet an hour early on Monday."

"No, alright," I said. "I'll see you then."

On the appointed evening I arrived at five to eight and discovered Chris, Dave and Barry huddled in a group around the corner table. They each gave me a nod as I came in, then continued talking while I ordered a drink at the bar. The pub was relatively quiet, and I overheard part of their conversation.

"He's either that," murmured Chris, "or sort of, like, you know, he thinks, 'I'll be groovy', you know."

I glanced across at them and they all began to look rather sheepish.

"Who are they talking about?" said George. "You or me?"

Evidently he'd overheard them too.

"Neither," I replied. "It's a highly obscure reference, known only to a small circle of followers."

George shook his head.

"They've been waiting here since seven o'clock," he said. "Haven't they got anything better to do?"

"Probably not," I replied.

At that moment the pub door swung open and Mike marched in. When he saw me he came straight over.

"Hey!" he said, waving a record in my face. "You didn't tell me about this!"

"What is it?" I asked.

"'Eight Miles High'," he proclaimed. "Three minutes thirty-five seconds."

I put my finger to my lips and drew him aside.

"Yes, well, I should keep it to myself if I were you," I said, in an undertone. "We never know who might be listening."

It was eight o'clock, so I hustled him into the back room where James had just finished setting up. We were swiftly pursued by Chris, Dave and Barry. There was also a newcomer, a guy I'd noticed loitering near the bar with a telltale package in his hand. His name was Rupert, and we all did our best to make him feel welcome. Vaguely I noted that once again the man in the long, leather coat had failed to appear, but after that he faded from my mind.

The additional hour afforded by the early start seemed to create an expansive mood amongst the seven of us. A promising evening lay ahead, and as we awaited the first record an air of anticipation filled the room. It was customary for new recruits to begin proceedings, and Rupert's opening selection was "Conscious Man". He looked slightly bemused when nobody showed any reaction to it, but was soon reconciled once James had explained the rules. Dave came next with "On the Road Again", then Barry chose "Born To Be Wild", while my offering was "Mr Brightside". As we moved around the table towards Mike I noticed he was becoming increasingly tense, as if impatient to present his first choice. He remained visibly agitated until "Eight Miles High" was laid on the deck and the needle sank into the groove, after which he loosened up considerably. Chris followed this up nicely with "Get Me to the World on Time," then James completed the opening round by playing "Waterloo Sunset". We listened closely until the final notes dwindled into oblivion and the record ceased turning. Eventually, Chris broke our silent reverie:

" 'Terry and Julie cross over the river, where they feel safe and sound.' "

James nodded his head but said nothing, and it struck me as rather odd that he allowed Chris these weekly utterances. The rules clearly stated that there were to be no comments or judgements, yet Chris regularly flouted the convention without censure. On the other hand I suppose it could be argued that quoting directly from a song infringed neither category, and I have to admit that personally I harboured no objection to the practice. Chris had a very gentle voice and his delivery was barely intrusive. Moreover, he had an extraordinary ability to distil the essence of a song into a single line. Whenever he spoke, we all understood exactly what he meant. Well, most of us did anyway.

Mike pondered the words for a moment or two, and then asked, "Who's Terry and Julie?"

Nobody even tried to explain.

"If you weren't there," said Barry, "you wouldn't know."

"Well, I wasn't," replied Mike, "so I don't."

It was time for the next round of music, and Rupert's second contribution was "Pressure Drop". Dave followed this with "Seven Seas", and Barry chose "Into the Valley". The evening was beginning to flow very smoothly and I was impressed by the wide variety of sounds we were sharing with one another. As a consequence the hours drifted by wholly unobserved. There was a brief wobble in proceedings when Mike announced that he wished to present "Eight Miles High" for each of his three turns (he'd actually brought no other records with him), but after due consideration James gave his consent.

"We'll let it go just this once," he informed Mike. "Next week please try to bring three different choices."

Soon we moved on to the final round, and Rupert handed James a copy of "Long Shot Kick the Bucket". After that came "The Story of the Blues", and while it was playing I happened to glance towards the door, which I noticed was slightly ajar. Presumably it had slipped off its latch. Or maybe not. Outside in the darkened passageway stood a slender young woman cautiously peeping in at us. When she caught my gaze she moved back into the shadows a little. A few seconds later she peeped in again, so I tapped James on the arm and alerted him to her presence. He continued listening until the record had faded away, and then he spoke.

"We appear to have an eavesdropper," he said. "Close the door, will you?"

The instruction was directed at me (as usual) so I rose from my chair and went across to the doorway. The girl's eyes met mine as I approached, and I saw them flash with anger when I shut her out. I heard the clatter of enraged footsteps retreating down the passageway, then I returned to my place at the table feeling rather remorseful.

"She'll have to come back next week," remarked James, before turning his attention once again to the red portable.

When the session ended we found to our amazement that it was almost eleven o'clock. Quickly we packed everything away and headed into the bar for a well-earned pint (or hopefully two). Immediately we saw that during the evening a new poster had been put up on the wall beside ours.

CONFESSIONAL RECORDS SOCIETY
MEETS HERE EVERY TUESDAY
9PM
BRING A RECORD OF YOUR CHOICE AND CONFESS!

"Oh yes," said Dave when he saw it, "I meant to tell you, I got a leaflet in the post from them."

"Me too," said Barry.

According to George, somebody had turned up about ten o'clock to make arrangements.

"By the way," he added, "they want to know if it's alright to borrow your record player."

"Certainly not," replied James with irritation. "They can bring their own."

"It'll save you having to move yours," George pointed out.

"I don't care," said James. "They're not borrowing it and that's that."

"Suit yourself."

This meant, of course, that James had to find somewhere to put the red portable until the following Monday. Understandably, George was reluctant to get involved any further, and only after much gentle persuasion was he prevailed upon to make space for it in the cellar.

"Be careful when you're going down the steps," he told James. "They're very steep and the light's not very bright."

James was gone a good while, and when eventually he emerged he had a question for George.

"Who was it who was asking anyway?"

"I didn't catch his name," George replied. "He only comes in occasionally. You know him: it's the chap who wears the long, leather coat."

"We don't really know him," I said. "We've only met him once."

George rang the bell for eleven o'clock, then carried on serving drinks.

"I've come to a decision," he announced. "There's no business for me if you all disappear into the back room for hours on end, so I'm going to open up the little bar on Monday evenings."

"Oh, right," said James. "Thanks."

"I've asked Alice to take charge."

"Who's Alice?" I enquired.

"She's the new barmaid," said George. "She was only meant to work Fridays and Saturdays but now she's agreed to help out Mondays too."

"Ah."

"Comes highly recommended."

"Really?"

"I told her to pop in and say hello this evening. I was busy and didn't have time for a formal introduction."

James glanced at me but made no comment.

"What about Tuesdays?" said Barry. "Are the 'confessionals' getting their own special bar as well?"

"Too soon to say," George answered. "They're only a one-man-band at present, so we'll have to wait and see how they develop."

"Anybody shown any interest?"

"Don't know," he said. "Like I told you: I was busy."

When I got home that night I went straight to my turntable and played "Baby, You're a Rich Man". As I sat and listened my thoughts went back to the day I bought the single all those years ago. The other side was supposed to have been recorded during a "live" world television transmission, though everybody knew it hadn't been really. Everybody, that is, except me: I always believed what it said on the label, and anyway

I'd seen the live broadcast with my own eyes. On that first day I played "Baby, You're a Rich Man" sixteen times in succession before my dad came in and told me enough was enough. As the memory subsided I wondered if this counted as a "confession". Could I take it to the Confessional Records Society and "confess" to my misdemeanour?

Or perhaps I'd misunderstood the concept entirely. Maybe people were forced to sit in an interrogation chair with a record playing repeatedly until they "confessed" to enjoying it. Probably not. More likely the society appealed to sentimental types who were easily reduced to tears, and who selected songs like "If You Leave Me Now" or "Can't Live Without You". Either that, or they were expected to share with all and sundry some excruciating detail of their personal life which a particular record reminded them of. It all sounded a very morbid prospect to me.

Nevertheless I was highly tempted to spy on the first meeting just to find out exactly what happened in there. Conceivably I could lurk in the passageway of the Half Moon and eavesdrop on proceedings.

While I was pondering all this "Baby, You're a Rich Man" finished and the turntable clicked off. At the same instant I realised that the word "eavesdrop" had made me feel rather queasy. For a moment I couldn't think why, and then I remembered the girl outside the door and the way her eyes had flashed with anger when I shut her out. I'd since discovered that her name was Alice; and it seemed I would have to face her the following Monday.

Until then, I decided, the best course of action was to steer clear of the Half Moon. This of course ruled out any idea of "spying" on the Confessional Records Society. Furthermore, when I considered the matter in detail, it struck me that rather than mock our rivals we should try and look to ourselves. After all, the Forensic Records Society was far from perfect. To start with I still had certain reservations about the rules, especially the prohibition on comments and judgements. It was all very well for James to apply the rigorous letter of the law, but I'd already noticed sporadic signs of resistance. In truth it was only with great restraint that Dave, Barry and Mike had suppressed their desire to speak. As I mentioned before, an exception was occasionally allowed when Chris repeated lines from various songs, yet this acted as little more than a safety valve on a simmering problem. Ultimately I feared that the whole operation might disintegrate under the pressure. Besides, I doubted if the term "forensic" was wholly appropriate if we weren't permitted to examine any of the records in detail. All we did was play them and put them away again. For James and me this arrangement had always been quite satisfactory, but I questioned how long the others would accept the situation. Finally there was the unexplained problem of the missing hours and minutes: despite our attempts to keep a close rein on the process, we persistently ran out of time. Obviously these were all concerns that I kept to myself, and I had no intention of raising them at subsequent meetings. Even so, they continued to hover in the background.

As it transpired, however, events were about to take an altogether different and unexpected turn.

I arrived at the Half Moon the following Monday and knew at once that something was amiss. Chris, Dave and Barry were gathered at their usual table in the corner, all peering earnestly at a fourth man who was standing talking to them. Their brows were furrowed, and then I saw that the newcomer was holding in his hands a bunch of long-playing records. He looked extremely disappointed, presumably because he'd just found out his journey had been wasted. The Forensic Records Society didn't cater for LPs and I guessed the other three had already broken the news to him. Judging by his forlorn expression he'd taken it rather badly. They were plainly in need of moral support, and when Barry spotted me he left the table and sauntered over.

"Do you think you could have a word with this guy?" he said quietly. "He seems to have come to the wrong place."

"Alright," I said. "Leave it to me."

I spotted an empty table and sat down, and a few moments later Barry directed the man towards me. Swiftly I debated what to say. He was still clutching his records, which fortunately provided me with a suitable opening. Even so, the task I faced was far from easy. It was my duty to explain to him that the society was still in its infancy and was therefore unprepared for long-players; secondly, that in our opinion LPs lacked the conciseness and immediacy of singles (our preferred medium); and, finally, that there simply wasn't enough time for long, drawn-out performances lasting ten, twelve or even fifteen minutes. I only hoped I could make him understand without causing any further upset. As soon as he spoke, though, I realised I'd completely misread the situation.

"I came here last Tuesday," he announced, "to try and join the Confessional Records Society."

"Oh yes?" I said.

"But they turned me away."

"Why was that then?"

"They said it was the wrong kind of confession."

"Ah."

Needless to say I was astounded by this disclosure. Not only did it strike me as preposterous that a newly established society should reject potential recruits, but also I was becoming increasingly baffled as to what they meant by "confession". Perhaps, I surmised, they didn't know themselves. The man standing in front of me obviously didn't, but at least I now had the chance to find out a little more about them, if only indirectly.

"Tell you what," I said. "You can confess to me if you like."

He glanced all around him.

"You mean here?" he asked.

"Yes."

"Isn't there a special room set aside for the purpose?"

"Not really, no."

"Oh," he said. "Well, yes, thank you. That certainly would be appreciated."

I indicated a chair opposite mine and he sat down. His name, apparently, was Keith.

"So what do you want to confess?" I enquired.

"An episode from the past," he said. "Years ago I went on holiday to my auntie's house in Ireland and one morning while I was having a bath I started singing 'Happiness is a Warm Gun' and when I came out of the bathroom my auntie smacked me."

"Why?"

"She said I'd been rude about the Mother Superior."

"Jumping the gun?"

"Yes."

Keith fell silent and sat gazing across the table.

"Is that it?" I asked.

"Yes."

"Were you alone in the bath?"

"Yes."

"And was this when you were a child?"

"No," said Keith. "It was when I was a grown-up."

I considered the story for a minute or so.

"Sounds like a reasonable confession to me," I said at length.

"That's what I thought," replied Keith.

"But the other society rebuffed you?"

"Correct."

A related question then occurred to me.

"How many of them were there?" I asked. "Roughly."

"In the other society?"

"Yes."

"Three," he said. "Three men."

The pub door swung open and Mike came in, followed closely by Rupert. A glance at the clock told me it was five to eight. I rose to my feet and gave Keith an encouraging nod.

"Well," I said, "I hope that's been of some help to you."

"Yes, thank you," he answered. "Like a pint?"

"Oh, it's quite unnecessary."

"It's the least I can do," he insisted. "Pint of Guinness, is it?"

"Er . . . yes. Thanks."

"Right," he said. "I'll have to be quick; it's nearly time to go in."

This last remark came as a surprise, because I'd been expecting Keith to head straight for home once he'd made his confession. Now it seemed he planned to join us, which put me in a very awkward position. I didn't have the heart to tell him he couldn't bring his long-playing records into the meeting, especially now he was buying me a pint.

Under the circumstances I decided my best bet was to go through to the back room and apprise James of what was happening. I was sure he'd know what to do, so I casually slipped away. However, when I tried the door at the end of the passage I found it was locked. I knocked and waited. There was no reply. I knocked again and this time the door opened by an inch and the barmaid peered out. The instant she laid eyes on me she closed it again. I knocked for a third time and after a long delay she opened up once more.

"What?" she demanded.

"I need to speak to James."

"Well, you can't," she said. "He's busy."

Now a second voice spoke from somewhere within. It belonged to James.

"Who is it, Alice?" he asked.

"Nobody," she answered, closing the door again.

The hour was very nearly eight o'clock and I could hear the others coming. In desperation I knocked a bit harder, but to no avail. A few seconds later I was joined by Mike and Rupert.

"Evening," said Mike, giving the door a friendly tap. Immediately it opened and he led the way inside. Next came Rupert, and then Chris and Dave. Behind them was Keith, carrying a pint in each hand and his long-players tucked beneath his arm. After they'd all filed past me Barry appeared. He was holding back a little and looked rather displeased.

"I thought you were going to sort this out," he murmured as he went by. "It's all highly improper."

I shrugged and followed him into the room, where James was presiding over the red portable. He was observing everybody as they came in, and I saw him glance briefly at Keith's records. Alice, meanwhile, stood waiting in silent attendance behind the corner bar. She acknowledged none of us, but instead stared impassively over our heads.

People were already taking their places around the table, and I saw that Keith had saved a chair for me.

"Thanks," I said, settling down beside him.

James was sitting opposite, quietly assessing the situation. He'd plainly grasped that there'd been a misunderstanding, and when he began his opening remarks he was careful to employ diplomatic language.

"Well," he said, "we seem to have an irregularity."

"Yes," I replied, "but on this occasion it can probably be overlooked."

"On what grounds?"

"Humanitarian."

"Huh," said Barry.

A muted grunt from Dave suggested that he, too, was in disagreement. Nonetheless, James had known me long enough to detect the urgency of my implied appeal. He responded by reaching over to the red portable and changing the speed to 33rpm.

Keith, of course, remained totally oblivious to the ideological dispute that was seething all around him. He sat innocently behind his small stack of long-players waiting for the meeting to start, and looked pleasantly surprised when he was asked to do the honours.

"Right," said James, addressing him directly, "as the newest member you're entitled to begin proceedings."

"Oh," said Keith. "Thanks."

"Can you hand me your first selection please?"

Now it was my turn to look surprised. In view of Keith's recent confession I'd assumed he would present "Happiness is a Warm Gun" for his opening choice. The famous double gatefold jacket was actually lying at the top of his stack, so I was astonished when he slid an entirely different record from underneath and passed it over. This also had a gatefold jacket, but there the similarity ended. I watched in stunned disbelief as

James laid the long-player on the turntable and lowered the arm.

"Disgraceful," said Barry.

"Outrageous," said Dave.

"As a matter of fact it's 'Out-Bloody-Rageous'," said Keith. "Nineteen minutes ten seconds."

"Really?" uttered Mike, clearly impressed by the information.

"The fade-in alone extends to almost five minutes," Keith added.

"Blimey."

The record started and I breathed a sigh of relief. We'd reached a crucial juncture, and Mike's evident interest in Keith's offering had served as a useful distraction from the impending crisis. Barry and Dave were on the verge of rebellion, but they'd been temporarily forestalled. Convention obliged them to desist from comment or judgement once the record had begun. Instead they sat and listened with indignant rage to the sound of a disjointed keyboard emerging very gradually out of the static. This took an extraordinarily long time and meanwhile they really had no alternative than to drink their beer and make the most of it.

As the instrumental wended its way onward, I wondered if the future of the Forensic Records Society would hinge on this particular piece of music. I sincerely hoped it wouldn't because I thoroughly enjoyed our Monday evenings in the back room of the Half Moon. On the surface everything seemed quite normal. We sat around the table in our various attitudes (serene, solemn, mesmerised and so forth) and there were no obvious signs of discontent. I knew, however, that Dave and Barry were far from satisfied with the current arrangements, and I was unsure about the others. Mike concentrated so intently on each record that he appeared to be concentrating on "concentrating", but otherwise he was unreadable. Chris and Rupert were equally opaque (I'd seen Chris raise his eyebrows once or twice but that was all). Yet it was plain that the society needed to adapt in order to survive. From its earliest inception we'd decided on an "organic" approach, and it occurred to me that maybe we'd allowed it to evolve too quickly. Perhaps, for example, the original template devised by James had been unduly rigid and required subtle alterations. His edict forbidding comments or judgements certainly put paid to any valid "deconstruction" of recordings through informed discussion. On the other hand there'd never been a specific ban on long-players, and this oversight threatened to open the floodgates. Seen from an overall perspective the society's constitution had been severely weakened: indeed, to judge by Dave and Barry's reaction a split was more than likely.

As I sat contemplating these problems I noticed I'd practically drained my glass of Guinness. It was unusual for me to drink it so swiftly and I concluded that my doubts and reservations must have made me especially thirsty. Not to worry, though: there were still several minutes before "Out-Bloody-Rageous" was due to finish, so I took the opportunity to buy another pint each for Keith and me. I left my seat and headed for the corner bar, forgetting for a moment who was in charge of it. Only when I was standing face-to-face with Alice did I remember, and by then it was too late. She regarded me sternly as I attempted my best smile.

"Two pints of Guinness please," I said.

Her response was to turn away and take two empty glasses from the shelf before slowly filling them. The process took two or three minutes, during which she neither spoke to me nor looked in my direction. This was possibly because she was applying herself wholly to the task, but I suspected it was more likely a demonstration of outright contempt for me. My theory was confirmed when I came to pay for the drinks.

"Thanks," I said, handing her some cash.

Again she said nothing, and when she returned with the change she put it on the counter rather than placing it in my hand. Finally she moved away and began tidying the shelves. As I carried the drinks to the table I realised it was going to take some time to get on the right side of her.

"Out-Bloody-Rageous" eventually ended and James removed it from the turntable. Now that it was over I expected to hear a storm of protest from Barry and Dave, but to my surprise there was none, not even a flurry. Instead, Barry expressed his dissent by handing James a copy of "This Town Ain't Big Enough for Both of Us". Dave followed with "Anyone Can Make a Mistake" and after that the meeting resumed its former civilised tone. Mike's offering was "Ain't Got a Clue" and Rupert chose "Redemption Song"; James was next with "Won't Get Fooled Again" while Chris contributed "You Can't Always Get What You Want". I completed the first round by selecting "Do Anything You Wanna Do" and then, of course, it was Keith's turn again. I watched in consternation as he produced yet another double gatefold sleeve from his stack.

"You'll like this," he announced. " 'Several Species of Small Furry Animals Gathered Together in a Cave and Grooving with a Pict'."

Keith's unwitting but repeated contravention of the rules at last stirred James into action.

"Oh, by the way," he said. "We don't allow any comments or judgements."

"Sorry," came the reply. "Won't happen again."

I waited for James to mention long-players as well, but for some reason he didn't. He merely took the record from Keith and placed it on the deck. A few seconds later the sound of a fly being swatted signalled the start of "Several Species of Small Furry Animals Gathered Together in a Cave and Grooving with a Pict". Once more we had no alternative other than to sit and listen.

While the track was playing Chris went over to the bar for another beer; then Mike and Rupert; then Barry and Dave; and I noticed Alice was charming to all of them. Her disdain was apparently reserved for me alone. At the same time, however, I sensed that each of us was somehow under close observation. When she wasn't serving drinks she adopted a detached manner as she busied herself with various minor duties. Even so, I could tell that she was fully absorbing all the goings-on around the table; not only the different choices we made, but also the brief exchanges between us. Alice took everything on board, not least the fact that James was founder of the Forensic Records Society and therefore the supreme presence to whom we deferred. It wasn't until long after that I discovered the significance of her accumulated knowledge.

Keith's record was now drawing towards its climactic ending, and we listened in awe as the deranged voice ranted and raved and ultimately died away. A few more seconds went by, and then Chris broke the silence:

"That was pretty avant-garde, wasn't it?"

It was all he said, but we knew exactly what he meant.

Most of us did anyway.

"Hang on a sec!" exclaimed Mike. "I was told we weren't allowed to make comments or judgements!"

"You aren't," James replied, "but in this case it was neither one nor the other."

"What was it then?"

"A quotation."

"Well I didn't hear it."

"I'm not surprised," said James. "It requires the right kind of ears."

I had no idea whether the remark was supposed to be an insult or a piece of helpful advice, but whatever the intention it rendered Mike momentarily speechless. Meanwhile, Barry was becoming increasingly exasperated. It was his turn to present the next record, but instead of handing his selection to James he withheld it until he had everybody's attention. When at last he spoke his tone was grave.

"It seems to me," he said, "that there's different rules for different people."

"Quite," said Dave.

A hush fell over the entire gathering.

"How do you mean?" James asked.

"Well, I don't wish to cause any upset," said Barry, "but I always assumed we favoured singles over long-players."

"Correct," James answered. "We do."

"Do we?" declared Keith, plainly taken aback.

"I'm afraid so," said James, "but you weren't to know."

"No, I didn't," said Keith. "Sorry."

"My fault," I said. "I should have told you after you confessed."

No sooner had I spoken than I regretted it. Across the table James glanced at me sharply.

"I thought we were going to have nothing to do with confessions," he said. "That's what we agreed."

"It was supposed to be private," Keith added. "Just between me and you."

In different ways, they both looked as if they felt deeply betrayed. Silence filled the room. Many eyes were upon me and I was beginning to feel very uncomfortable, but fortunately Dave rode to my rescue.

"I've got a confession," he said flatly, "if anybody wants to hear it."

I watched as James quickly weighed up the situation. The meeting had ground to a halt for a variety of conflicting reasons, and Dave's offer appeared to provide a solution. Maybe this would clear the air a little.

"Alright," said James at length. "Go ahead."

There was a pause as Dave composed himself.

"Well," he said, "a long time ago I spent an evening with a fellow called Jeremy Woodhouse. I can't remember how I knew him or what I was doing in his tent but there were three other people present besides me and I got the strong impression they all wanted me to leave. So eventually I did, and just before I departed he told me about this record that had just been released. He said I should check it out because it was probably the best record I would ever hear."

Dave paused again.

"Is that your confession?" asked James.

"No," Dave replied. "My confession is that I didn't listen to it for another thirty years. Not properly anyway."

"What was the record?"

" 'Tears of a Clown'."

"And was he right about it?"

"I can't answer that," said Dave. "We're not allowed comments or judgements."

"Have you got a copy with you?"

"Yes."

"Well let's play it now then."

It was actually Barry's turn next, but he voiced no objection so Dave handed over his record and we spent the next few minutes listening to "Tears of a Clown". After that the session resumed as normal.

50

Now he'd made his point, Barry seemed content to let matters lie (at least for the moment). The same applied to everyone else. They sat at the table in their various attitudes (serene, solemn, mesmerised and so forth) and continued applying themselves to the art of listening. By the time we reached the final round we'd heard an infinite variety of recordings from countless sources. Keith presented "Happiness is a Warm Gun" and the rest of us followed with our respective selections. The society, I decided, was functioning as well as might be expected considering all the different views people held. Any perceived faults could be adjusted organically in due course. My only misgiving was the incident over Keith's confession. I earnestly hoped it hadn't soured relations between me and James.

As the evening drew to a close, Alice moved from behind the bar and began collecting empty glasses. She was wearing platform shoes, and I was vaguely pondering how on earth she managed to walk in them when suddenly a more urgent thought occurred to me. I reflected on the protracted records we'd heard, and the interruptions we'd suffered, and I realised that it must be very late indeed. Any second I expected George to come barging through the door and threaten us with eviction. Oddly enough, though, nobody else looked the slightest bit bothered, and when at last we emerged from the meeting I discovered it was only twenty to eleven.

"Plenty of time yet," observed George in a genial manner.

51

"Your clock's correct then, is it?" I asked.

"Never been wrong," he replied. "Oh, by the way, the chap in the long, leather coat was here making enquiries again. He wanted to know how many members you had."

"Did you tell him?"

"Of course," said George. "It's not a secret, is it?"

"Suppose not."

"Bit of a cheek all the same."

"Why?"

"Because I gave him the information he wanted and then he only bought a glass of soda water."

"Yes, you're right," I said. "Cheek."

The prospect of financial profit reminded George about the other bar.

"I'll have to catch Alice when she comes through," he remarked. "I need to start cashing up."

There was no sign of her at present, and it turned out that she and James were still tidying the back room. I glanced around to see what everybody else was doing. Over at the corner table Barry, Chris, Rupert and Keith were deep in conversation about some matter of seemingly great importance. Meanwhile, Mike had taken Dave aside to discuss a separate issue.

"No, no," Dave was saying, "the guy didn't suggest it was perfect: he said it was probably the best record I would ever hear."

"How long is it?" Mike asked.

"Don't know," said Dave. "Why do you ask?"

"Well," said Mike, "the benchmark for perfection is three minutes precisely."

"Then I'd say it was pretty close," Dave replied.

"What about 'The Tracks of my Tears'?"

"That's quite a different subject."

I left the pair of them comparing notes and went to join the group in the corner. They all ceased talking as I sat down, and for a moment I thought I was possibly unwelcome. Perhaps the earlier incident was still fresh in their memories. Next instant, however, I realised the true cause of their abrupt lapse into silence. Alice had just come out of the back room followed by James, who was carrying the red portable. She held the door open for him as he descended the stairs to the cellar, then went and assisted George behind the bar.

"Blimey," said Keith. "How on earth does she manage to walk in those shoes?"

It was a question none of us could answer.

When James came back upstairs he looked rather distracted. He sat down with us but said so little he might as well have been on another planet, and I guessed he was still contemplating the various problems that had arisen during the meeting. Paramount, of course, was the unexplained riddle of the clock. When originally we formed the society our stated intention had been to play records under controlled conditions according to a strict timetable. For various reasons this plan had quickly gone by the board, so that meetings never finished quite when we expected them to. Personally I found the experience left me feeling slightly disorientated, and I presumed James was similarly affected.

Eventually, though, he pulled himself together.

"Right," he snapped, rising to his feet. "See you all at eight o'clock next week."

He gathered up his records and left without another word. A short while later George rang the bell.

"Can I just check?" said Keith. "LPs are prohibited, aren't they?"

"Correct," I replied.

"Also comments and judgements," added Barry.

"Right."

"Come on you lot!" barked George. "Out!"

There was no excuse to remain any longer, so at last we started leaving. From my point of view it was an inauspicious departure. Alice was still helping clear up behind the bar, and as we filed past she wished everyone goodnight except me. Outside it was cold and rainy, but I set off walking undeterred. I finally reached home having made up my mind not to be troubled too much by Alice's repeated snubs. Instead I switched my attention to an idea that had occurred to me during the evening. It entailed an extensive period of research which was to keep me occupied until the small hours. Even so it would be well worth the effort. Somewhere in my collection was an item that promised to be of particular interest to a certain member of the Forensic Records Society. When eventually I found what I was seeking I set it carefully aside.

It was now very late indeed, but I had one more task to perform. Before going to bed I went over to my turntable and played "Who Knows Where the Time Goes?" After several successive listens I concluded that this was yet another question none of us could answer.

When I arrived at the Half Moon the following Monday I knew at once that something was amiss. Barry, Dave, Chris, Mike and Rupert were assembled around the usual corner table while James and Keith sat some distance away, apparently engaged in profound conversation. The clock said ten to eight, so I bought a pint and hovered near the bar, waiting to see how matters unfolded. Both James and Keith looked extremely pensive, and for a minute I wondered whether Keith was making a further "confession". If so, it would be an additional burden for James to carry on his shoulders. Hadn't he got enough to cope with already? It was imperative that somebody else should offer to share the load, but after the previous episode I felt reluctant to get involved again. For this reason I decided to stay just where I was and mind my own business.

As soon as he spotted me, however, James spoke quietly to Keith, then beckoned me over to join them.

"Glad you're here," he said. "Keith has suffered an unfortunate turn of events."

"Really?"

"It happened when I was out last night," Keith explained. "A man came round to the house and told my mother he was from the Confessional Records Society."

"Was he recruiting?" I enquired.

"No," replied Keith. "He claimed he'd met me before and asked my mother if he could have a look through my records."

"What!" I said with disbelief. "It's private!"

"I know."

"Don't tell me she said yes."

"I'm afraid so," said Keith. "Oh, I'm not blaming her. She's as much a victim as I am."

"Are there any records missing?" I asked.

"Not as far as I can tell."

"That's a relief."

"Nevertheless I feel as if I've been violated."

"I'm not surprised."

The visitor, it transpired, had examined Keith's collection for almost an hour. At one point his mother even offered to make him a cup of tea, but he declined. Poor Keith was quite distraught and it was clearly going to take him some time to recover. Understandably I was furious on his behalf. Who did the Confessional Records Society think they were, exactly, subjecting him to such torment? More importantly, what measures could we take to ensure such an intrusion was never repeated?

James glanced at the clock, then spoke to me.

"Could you do me a favour?" he said. "Can you go into the back room and see if Alice has everything ready?"

"Well," I replied, "I can if you like, but wouldn't it be better if you went?"

James gave me the same sharp look he'd given me the previous week when he thought I'd betrayed him.

"I can't leave Keith in this state!" he announced. "He needs help!"

As if to confirm the fact, Keith peered at me with desolation in his eyes.

56

"Er . . . oh . . . yes," I said. "Yes, you're right. I'll go at once."

"You'll probably have to start the meeting without me," James added.

I really had no option but to do as he asked, despite the frosty reception I was bound to receive from Alice. I quickly decided that the best way to disarm her was to adopt a casual manner and simply breeze into the back room as if relations between us were perfectly normal. Regrettably it didn't work.

Alice was just closing the lid of the red portable as I swung open the door and entered.

"Hello!" I said (breezily).

Instead of answering immediately, she busied herself straightening out a couple of chairs before moving away and slipping behind the corner bar. Finally she turned and faced me.

"I don't know what you're doing here," she said. "You don't even like music."

Alice uttered the words with such certainty that for a moment I was completely thrown off balance. An accusation as harsh as this had never previously been levelled at me and I was at a loss how to respond. Needless to say the charge was absurd and could not be substantiated. Yet neither could it be disproved, which meant I was more or less obliged to mount some kind of defence.

"Of course I like music."

"No you don't," said Alice.

"Yes I do."

"No you don't."

"But I listen to it all the time!"

"Makes no difference."

"You mean you don't like my choices?"

"That isn't what I said."

"Well if I don't like music," I demanded, "how come the others have never pointed it out?"

Alice stood regarding me in silence from behind the corner bar. Her face was expressionless, but when eventually she spoke her reply was crushing:

"Because they haven't seen through you."

Once again I was thrown off balance, and as I searched for a suitable riposte the door opened and Mike walked into the room, followed closely by Rupert, Chris, Dave and Barry.

"Sorry to interrupt," said Mike, "but it's almost eight o'clock."

Some of them wanted to buy drinks, so I readily made space for them at the bar. It was a welcome respite from the onslaught. I was hardly eager to continue my conversation with Alice, seeing I'd fared so badly, but at the same time I knew the matter wasn't settled. I'd been seriously shaken by the exchange and for a few seconds I stood apart from the others feeling awkward and isolated. My attempt at being "casual" was revealed to be an outright failure. For reasons of her own Alice had declared war against me, and her opening shot had knocked me to the floor. I actually wished I could disappear into thin air, but circumstances made escape impossible. There was no sign of James (or Keith) which meant it was my duty to take over the society's reins temporarily. Thankful for at least having something to do, I went and sat down in the chair nearest the red portable. I allowed myself a moment or two to regain my composure, then carefully raised the lid. To my mild surprise there was a record already lying on the turntable. It had a plain white label, completely blank except for the figures 4/25 handwritten in ink. This suggested I was looking at an extremely limited pressing (possibly a demo). I was just about to lift it up and examine the other side when someone reached across and whisked the record away in a single movement. I glanced up in astonishment and saw Alice standing over me.

"I'll take that, thank you very much," she said, sliding the record into a cardboard sleeve.

I had no idea how she'd moved so rapidly from behind the corner bar, but as she stalked back to her station I noticed Chris and the rest of them staring at her in awe. They'd all fallen noticeably silent, but they started talking again when Alice resumed serving drinks. I then endeavoured to get the meeting underway.

"Alright," I said, "who wants to get us started?"

The decision about who went first was usually taken by James, and in consequence my question brought no immediate reply. It was enough, however, to propel everyone to their places around the table. Once they were all seated I asked them again.

"I don't mind starting," said Barry, "if nobody objects."

Nobody did, so he handed over a copy of "Here We Go Round the Mulberry Bush" and I put it on the deck. While the record was playing I pondered how anyone could judge whether somebody else liked music or not. The answer, of course, was that it was impossible. The allegation was preposterous, and especially so when the accused person was a confirmed member of a dedicated forensic records society! I determined, therefore, to put the whole thing out of my head.

Nonetheless I was aware of a wave of apprehension creeping over me as the session continued and my turn drew nearer. Working clockwise around the table it was Dave next, then Rupert and then me. I felt increasingly self-conscious about my submissions for the evening, knowing full well that Alice was observing proceedings from behind the bar. Indeed, I was in such a state I couldn't even remember what they were! I peered down at my small stack of records and was reassured by the sight of "She Bangs the Drums" lying on top. A surreptitious peek revealed "She Comes in the Fall" underneath, and instantly my doubts subsided. In both cases I knew I was on safe ground.

Dave had chosen "Dandelion", and while we were listening I was pleased to see James ushering Keith into the room. He looked a little better and we quickly found him a seat at the table. Alice then came over to ask him what he'd like to drink, informing him it was "on the house". Privately I imagined George taking a very dim view of such generosity, but I decided to keep my thoughts to myself. A nod from James told me to carry on in my role as temporary chairman, and after that the meeting coasted along quite nicely.

60

Mike had brought his usual batch of concise recordings. These included "Banking on Simon" (two minutes thirteen seconds) and "A New England" (two minutes seven). Seeing them reminded me of the extensive research I'd conducted a few nights earlier, and I felt a surge of triumph when my final turn arrived.

"Here you are, Mike," I said. "This should be of interest."

"What is it?" he asked.

"'Another Girl, Another Planet'," I replied. "Three minutes precisely."

"Blimey."

"Your search for perfection is over."

Mike seemed highly impressed by my words, but they earned a swift rebuke from James.

"Comments aren't allowed," he announced. "You really should know better."

"Sorry," I said.

"Can I see that?"

"Certainly."

I handed him the record and for several seconds he gazed intently at the label. It was hard to tell what he was thinking, but when he passed it back he wore the same distracted expression I'd seen on his face the week before. During the next three minutes we sat around the table in our various attitudes (serene, solemn, mesmerised and so forth) and afterwards there were no comments or judgements. The remainder of the session was uneventful and we emerged at eleven o'clock, just as George rang the bell.

I half-expected James to stay behind and help Alice with the tidying up, so I was slightly surprised when he appeared at my side.

"Can you drop by and see me tomorrow morning?" he asked quietly. "There's something I need to discuss with you."

"Sure," I replied. "Nothing serious, I hope?"

"It's hard to tell just yet."

"Oh."

"Right," he said. "I'm just going to pop back and help Alice tidy up."

"OK."

I didn't see any more of James on Monday evening, despite waiting well beyond closing time, and I spent the last few minutes in Mike's company. He had a question for me.

"What was the title of that record again?"

"'Another Girl, Another Planet'."

"'Another Girl, Another Planet'," he intoned. "Do you mind if I borrow it till next week?"

"Course not."

"Three minutes precisely?"

"Yep."

"Unbelievable."

At ten o'clock the following morning I went to see James. There was a fairly long delay before he opened the door.

"Ah," he said, when he saw me.

"You asked me to drop by."

"Yes."

Instead of inviting me into the kitchen for a cup of tea, as was usual mid-morning, he directed me straight to his music room. He led me inside and told me to sit anywhere.

"Want a cup of tea?" he asked. "I've just made a pot."

"Er . . . yes, please," I said. "Are we having it in here?"

"Yes," he replied. "I'll only be a minute."

He left me alone in the room and closed the door behind him. The house was a haven of stillness. I chose a chair by the window and gazed around at the familiar rows of Schweppes boxes and laden shelves, before glancing at the forty-watt amplifier and deck. I noticed there was a record on the turntable with a plain white label, completely blank except for some figures handwritten in ink. Sheer curiosity urged me to go over and examine it more closely, but for a short while I resisted the temptation. James and I had an unwritten agreement which forbade us from looking through each other's records without being invited. When I thought about it properly, however, I decided that this case was different because the record was already on display. I rose from my chair, crossed the room and read the figures 4/25 on the label. At the same moment the door opened, so I stepped quickly to the window and peered out.

"Spring's on the way," I remarked.

"Really?" said James.

He was carrying a tea-tray loaded with cups and saucers, and some biscuits on a plate.

"Your favourite," he declared. "Malted Milk."

We sat down and he handed me my tea.

"Right," he said. "You're probably wondering why I asked you here."

"Just a little."

"Well, I'm rather disturbed by our friends in the Confessional Records Society."

"Oh yes?"

"They're behaving more and more unreasonably."

"Quite."

"So I think we ought to find out what they're up to."

James was of the opinion that the CRS (as he called them) had gone too far in their recent treatment of Keith. He therefore proposed that someone should attempt to infiltrate them and then report back to the rest of us.

"The person I have in mind," James explained, "should appear wholly guileless so as to be acceptable to the CRS, yet at the same time he must be immune to malign influences. In other words he needs to be straightforward and incorruptible."

"Do you mean me?" I asked.

"No," said James, "I mean Mike."

"Oh."

"From what I've seen he fills both categories."

"Yes, I suppose he does."

Apparently James had already made contact with Mike and intended to brief him before the next meeting of the Confessional Records Society.

"But that's tonight," I said.

"Yes, I know," James answered. "I'm afraid he's being thrown in at the deep end with hardly any preparation. There's even a risk they might try to convert him to their cause, but it's a chance we'll have to take."

"Does anybody else know about this?" I enquired.

"Not outside our immediate circle," said James. "I think it's best to keep it amongst ourselves until we've heard Mike's report."

"Is he going alone?"

"Oh yes."

"Very commendable of him."

"And I suggest we all keep well clear of the Half Moon until next Monday evening."

"Right."

Traditionally when I visited James he played me a record or two prior to my departure. It was a custom which had prevailed for many years, and which had figured as an important part in our lives. I recalled, for example, that the first time I ever heard "See Emily Play" was in James's music room. Likewise, a decade later it was me who introduced him to "Where Were You?" In both instances we shared something original and it created a kind of bond between us. This morning, however, I sensed a change. I'd been hoping to hear the mysterious record that was lying on his turntable, but for some reason the opportunity never arose. James merely gathered up the cups and saucers and put them on the tea-tray. Next thing I knew I was being shown into the hallway. Seemingly the long-lasting custom had been summarily broken, which I thought was a great shame.

He was still carrying the tray, and I noticed the kitchen door was closed.

"Shall I hold it open?" I enquired.

James paused a second before answering.

"No, no," he said. "I can manage, thanks."

"Alright, well I'll see you next Monday then."

"OK."

The house remained quiet as we said our goodbyes, but I couldn't help thinking there was someone waiting behind the kitchen door.

I spent the rest of Tuesday preoccupied by a number of misgivings. Not only had James been oddly unforthcoming, but there was also the prospect of Mike facing the Confessional Records Society entirely on his own. I pondered how he would cope when he was placed "on the spot" by the other members and then made to explain his selection. The injunction on their posters and leaflets was unambiguous: BRING A RECORD OF YOUR CHOICE AND CONFESS! It sounded to me as if the society was reaching out to people who were ashamed of the choices they made; or who perhaps led a furtive existence where they could only listen to music in secret. Whatever the reason, I suspected Mike was in for a difficult evening. By mid-afternoon I'd come to the conclusion that he was in serious need of moral support, and I then began debating the idea of going to the Half Moon in case he ran into any unpleasantness. Obviously I had no intention of gatecrashing the meeting, but I decided that no harm would be done if I looked into the pub about ten o'clock to check Mike was alright.

Furthermore, it occurred to me that there'd be no possibility of bumping into anybody else from the Forensic Records Society because James had advised everyone to keep away. With the coast clear, I could ease my worries over a pint of Guinness. That was the plan anyway.

When I walked into the Half Moon at ten o'clock the bar was unattended. I presumed George was in the cellar performing some duty or other, so I loitered patiently until he came back. A glance around the place told me business was thriving. All the tables and chairs were occupied and I noticed, unusually, that the clientele consisted wholly of women. They sat in groups, gossiping loudly and clutching in their hands pink numbered tickets of the type issued at cheese counters in supermarkets. Occasionally one of them would peer at the doorway leading to the back room, and it gradually dawned on me that they were waiting to go in. Considering it was a Tuesday evening the turnout was remarkable (much better than the Forensic Records Society ever managed) but it struck me they were starting rather late. I then realised I could hear music playing in the back room. It was only faint, yet I barely took a moment to recognise the distinctive tones of "Another Girl, Another Planet".

The meaning of all this information was still sinking in when I heard somebody ascending from the cellar. In the circumstances it was a very welcome sound. I was now desperately in need of a drink; I also looked forward to a reassuring dose of George's gruffness. Oddly, though, the approaching footsteps were much

67

lighter than the publican's weary plod, and a few seconds later expectation gave way to shock as Alice appeared at the top of the stairs. She was carrying a carton of wine glasses, having seemingly run out of them due to the large influx of women. Vaguely I remembered George mentioning weeks earlier that he was going to have to take a night off to attend a meeting of the Licensed Victuallers Association. I guessed that the night in question had duly arrived and that Alice was his chosen stand-in. After placing the carton on the end of the counter, she turned around to see if anyone wanted serving. When she saw me her face darkened.

"Come to confess, have you?" she enquired.

"Confess what?" I replied.

"You know exactly what I mean."

"No I don't," I said. "Pint of Guinness please."

With ill-disguised scorn she moved away and began filling a glass. Meanwhile, the record playing in the back room was rapidly nearing its conclusion. I listened as best I could as it stuttered to a halt. There then followed a brief hiatus during which I thought I heard raised voices, but the constant hubbub surrounding me made it impossible to tell what was being said. All of a sudden Mike emerged from the back room carrying a record and headed directly for the exit. His face looked extremely pale.

"Mike!" I called, but he paid me no attention.

Having just ordered a pint I was reluctant to go in pursuit of him, so I remained where I was and settled down on a bar stool to see how events unfolded. A minute or so after Mike's hurried departure I sensed a wave of anticipation passing amongst the groups of women.

"Here's Phillip," said one of them.

Out of the back room walked the man in the long, leather coat.

"Who's next?" he asked.

"Me," replied a blonde woman near me. "Number eleven."

"Come along then."

It took her several seconds to gather her belongings, and while he waited the man cast his eyes over the animated throng. An instant later his gaze met mine. He stared at me coldly before turning his attention once more to the blonde woman. I thought she looked rather apprehensive as he led her into the back room and closed the door.

"So his name's Phillip," said somebody nearby. "At least you know that much about him."

I glanced around just as Alice placed my pint on the bar.

"No," I protested. "That's not why I'm here at all."

"Really?"

I detected a note of mistrust in her voice, but I decided I was under no obligation to explain myself so I said nothing else and paid for my drink with the exact money. Just then I heard a record start up in the back room. It was "The Day Before You Came", and while it was playing I wondered what could have gone wrong with Mike's confession. He'd appeared highly distressed when he left the Half Moon and I was beginning to regret not going after him when I had the chance. On the other hand I was slightly cross about his choice of record. Presumably it was my copy of "Another Girl, Another Planet" that he'd brought with him this evening, and I felt he really should have asked my permission first. Moreover, I wasn't absolutely sure if it was the sort of thing the Confessional Society was seeking. Something a little less abstract would probably have been more suitable; but then again who was I to judge? To tell the truth I was still quite perplexed by their methods and objectives. All I knew for sure was that Mike's attempt to penetrate them had failed at the first hurdle.

"The Day Before You Came" ended and after a few moments the blonde woman emerged from the back room. With some alarm I noticed she was in floods of tears, but I soon realised they were actually tears of joy. Her friends (also in tears) flocked around her offering their congratulations. Meanwhile, the next woman in the queue eagerly awaited her turn to confess. How different it all was to a typical meeting of the Forensic Records Society.

I was disinclined to stay any longer, so I finished my pint and prepared to leave. As I edged my way towards the door, however, the man in the long, leather coat reappeared. I tried to avoid his gaze, but when he saw me he moved swiftly to block my path.

"Not going so soon, are you?" he asked.

"Afraid so," I replied. "Sorry."

"Oh yes," he said, "you're always sorry, aren't you?"

"Pardon?"

"Your favourite word, isn't it?"

"Look," I said. "I don't know what you're talking about."

"You've nothing to confess then?"

"No!" I snapped. "I haven't!"

"Well, come back if you ever change your mind," he said. "We'll always be here for you."

With that he stepped aside and I headed for the door, fully aware that Alice had witnessed the entire exchange.

A few days later I received a memo from James informing me that an extraordinary meeting of the Forensic Records Society would be held the following Monday. Its purpose was to discuss "certain matters arising". In consequence there would only be time for one record apiece. The memo had apparently been circulated to all members.

On the appointed evening I arrived at five to eight and discovered Chris, Dave and Barry huddled in a group around the corner table. They each gave me a nod as I came in, then continued talking while I ordered a drink at the bar. The pub was relatively quiet, and I overheard part of their conversation.

" 'Essence of giraffe'," murmured Barry.

I glanced across at them and they all looked away.

"Who are they talking about?" said George. "You or me?"

Evidently he'd overheard them too.

"Neither," I replied. "It's a highly obscure reference. Nothing personal."

For my own reasons I decided not to join them. Instead I waited at the bar until Rupert, Keith and Mike arrived. I assumed James (and Alice) had already gone into the back room.

Eventually Mike approached me.

"You know the record I borrowed?" he asked. "Could I keep it another week?"

"Suppose so," I said. "You like it then, do you?"

"Of course," he said. "Perfect."

"Some people see it in a different way," I ventured.

"Yes."

"Too abstract for them."

"Maybe."

I peered at him enquiringly, but he said no more so I didn't pursue the issue further. No doubt it would all be resolved once the meeting began. A minute went by and the clock ticked around to eight o'clock; then we all trooped into the back room and sat down. James had set the red portable in its usual place, which I took as a positive sign. After all, the primary reason we came here was to play records, not talk. Nevertheless I supported the strategy James had put in motion. It was patently necessary for us to address the menace imposed by the Confessional Records Society. Our integrity was at stake and we could no longer simply ignore them. The priority, therefore, was to find out what had happened to Mike the previous Tuesday evening. Alice was in position behind the corner bar, and at James's suggestion Mike went and bought himself a stiff drink.

Meanwhile, James made an introductory speech.

"Now, as you know," he said, "we've lately been subjected to the unwanted attentions of the CRS. Why they wish to obtrude on us remains unfathomable, so after due consideration I asked Mike to try and discover what he could about their inner workings. Alright, Mike, when you're ready I'll leave you to take up the story."

By now Mike had got his drink (a bottle of strong lager) and returned to the table. He poured half the contents into a glass and swigged it down.

"Well," he began, "what they do is they come around beforehand taking a list of names."

"Sorry, Mike," James interrupted. "Who are 'they' exactly?"

"There's three of them," Mike answered. "The leader's this bloke in a long, leather coat called Phillip, and his two helpers are both called Andrew. Anyway, as I was saying, they come around beforehand with this list and take everybody's name, then you give them the record you've chosen and receive a pink numbered ticket. After that you have to wait until they call you."

"You mean you go in alone?" asked Barry.

"Correct," said Mike. "It's quite daunting."

"Good grief."

"It seems they've diverged from the classic American model," said James. "Over there everybody participates together."

"Not over here, though," remarked Barry.

"No," agreed James. "Not over here."

Mike took another swig of his lager.

"Once they've called you in," he continued, "Phillip takes charge. He sits you down in front of a hi-fi and plays your record; then you're supposed to tell the three of them why you like it. Trouble was, I didn't get very far."

"Why was that?" enquired James.

"Well I'd chosen 'Another Girl, Another Planet'," Mike replied, "but when I mentioned it was precisely three minutes long Phillip denounced me as a fake."

"What!" exclaimed Dave. "How dare he?"

"Don't know," said Mike, "but the two Andrews backed him up and next thing I knew I was being shown the door."

"Without explanation?"

"Yes."

Poor Mike looked pale and shaken from merely having to relive the experience. He quickly finished his lager and went over to the bar for another. When he came back James offered words of consolation.

"Don't worry," he said, "you're definitely not a fake."

"Thanks," said Mike.

There was a brief silence, finally broken by Keith.

"So why do you like it?" he asked.

He posed the question in all innocence and plainly meant no harm. Even so, I heard a gasp of shock from most of the others. Mike, I noticed, had turned even paler than before.

"You don't have to answer that question," James announced at length, "but in a way I'm glad Keith asked it. The point is that we in the Forensic Records Society are purists. We don't allow comments or judgements and that's why the notion of 'confession' is so alien to us. The act of listening is what's important; we're not searching for any inner meaning. For this reason we can rest assured. We have nothing to fear from the CRS because we occupy the moral high ground. All the same we must continue to be wary of them."

"Their approach makes me shudder," said Dave.

"Me too," said Barry.

An outbreak of babble amongst the entire gathering indicated we were unanimous in our concurrence. This in turn signalled that the "extraordinary" session was over and that normality could resume.

"OK," said James. "Anybody who wants drinks can get them now, and then we'll play some records."

The next few minutes saw a general rush to the bar.

Equally normal, needless to say, was Alice's hostility towards me. I went and bought a pint each for me and James, and the whole transaction took place in deadly silence. This I found somewhat disconcerting. I was unsure whether James was aware of the situation, but if he was he didn't show it.

Fortunately the Forensic Records Society acted as a powerful restorative, and once proceedings were underway I swiftly forgot my troubles and cares. Everyone had obeyed the instruction to bring only one record each, which meant we had plenty of time; we could listen to them at our leisure without worrying too much about the clock. As a reward for his services Mike was allowed the first go, and he obliged by handing James a copy of "(Don't Fear) The Reaper". (I discovered afterwards that the recording had a duration of five minutes five seconds; clearly Mike was beginning to branch out.)

My turn followed and I selected "Heroes and Villains". Next up was Barry, who'd chosen "Road Runner". After him came Dave. His choice was also called "Roadrunner".

"Just a coincidence," he insisted.

The songs were completely different, by different performers from different decades with different styles and employing different production techniques. Even the layout of the titles was different. I couldn't help suspecting, however, that Dave and Barry were engaged in some kind of game with one another. After giving it further thought I remembered that their selections had been "linked" on previous occasions too. When Dave chose "On the Road Again", for example, Barry chased it with "Born to be Wild". A coincidence maybe, but I had my doubts.

Nonetheless the two offerings were heard in respectful silence. James had indeed spoken the truth: the strength of the Forensic Records Society lay in the purity of its methods. We listened to records forensically, without comment or judgement. This was our doctrine, and it served as a great leveller.

Gradually we worked our way around the table, with Chris, Rupert and Keith all taking their turns. Last in line was James, and when I glanced in his direction I recognised the record lying before him. It had a plain white label and was inscribed with the figures 4/25. The mysterious record! All of a sudden I realised why James hadn't played it the other day when I visited him: he was obviously waiting to present it in the rarefied conditions of the Forensic Records Society. Ever since the early days he'd been opposed to the idea of "trial runs", and I was pleased to note he was still practising what he preached. In a way this added to the excitement. Obviously we had a treat in store and James was saving it until the end of the session. Just as his turn came, however, we were rudely interrupted. The door opened and George looked in.

"Come on, you lot!" he growled. "It's gone eleven o'clock."

"It can't be," said James.

"Yes, it can," George replied. "I've already rung the bell twice."

"Well, we didn't hear it."

Despite our protestations we knew there was no use in arguing with George. James quickly handed each of us our records before packing away the red portable; then we all made for the door. George didn't even allow anyone to stay behind and help Alice with the tidying up. He wanted us out of the back room and that was that. When we got into the main bar we peered at the clock in disbelief. Once again time had slipped past us unobserved.

"I've given up even trying to understand it," said James.

"Same here," I answered.

I could tell there was something else bothering him too. As the others dispersed he drew me aside.

"Can you drop by and see me tomorrow morning?" he asked quietly. "I'd like you to help me with an experiment."

"Certainly," I said. "Ten o'clock?"

"That'll be fine."

When I got home my first job was to put the evening's choice of record back in its proper place (my collection was filed in strict alphabetical order). I happened to notice that the sleeve didn't match the label, and only then did I realise I'd been given the wrong record: instead of "Heroes and Villains" I was holding a copy of "Looking For Lewis and Clark". This, I remembered, had been Keith's offering. The reason for the mix-up, of course, was George's sudden interruption of the meeting. I assumed James had been in such a hurry to pack everything away that he'd inadvertently switched the records. For a moment I was disquieted by the discovery because I had no idea where Keith lived, but then I decided he could probably be trusted to safeguard my precious record until the following week. In the meantime I retained his as collateral.

At ten o'clock next morning I went to see James. He greeted me rather coolly, I thought, and led me directly to his music room. Standing in the middle of the floor was a hard, wooden chair. Above it hung a bare light bulb.

"Sit down, will you?" he said.

Over on his turntable I could see a record with a pink label which I recognised immediately. I sat down on the chair and tried to make myself comfortable.

"Right," said James. "What I'd like you to do is confess."

I gazed at him in astonishment.

"Confess to what?" I demanded.

"I haven't told you yet."

"But . . ."

"I know the idea sounds unorthodox to your ears," he continued, "but it's imperative that we learn how the confessional mind functions."

"Ah," I said. "Is this the experiment you mentioned?"

"Correct," James answered. "Now, I've taken the liberty of choosing the subject of your confession beforehand. There's a certain record I know you're particularly fond of, so with your permission we'll begin with that."

He stepped across to the turntable and switched it on. Seconds later I heard the opening bars from "Man of the World". They were followed by a plaintive voice singing.

I signalled to James and he stopped the record.

"You don't think it's a bit too obvious for a confession?" I asked. "He's telling us about his life."

"No need to worry at this stage," said James. "Just let it play right through and then you can tell me your thoughts."

"OK."

He restarted the record and I listened carefully until the end. To tell the truth I didn't even need to listen. I knew every note and every word by heart. All the same

I never tired of hearing it. Finally the turntable came to a halt.

"So?" said James.

"Well," I said. "The best description would be pathos, I suppose."

"You mean poignancy?"

"Yes."

James regarded me in silence for several moments.

"That's not the reason you like it though, is it?" he said at length.

"No," I replied.

"What else then?"

"Marvellous ensemble performance."

"Agreed," he said, "but again that's not the reason."

"No."

I puffed out my cheeks and pondered long and hard. This business of "confessing" was actually quite difficult.

"What about the words?" prompted James.

"Oh, yes, of course," I said. "The words are excellent."

"Words have never been your chief interest though, have they?" said James. "They're much more Chris's territory than yours."

"S'pose."

I began to sense that James was trying to "lead" me in a particular direction with his line of questioning. If this was indeed the case, then I was being rather slow on the uptake. In desperate search of inspiration I glanced at the record lying motionless on the turntable, and all of a sudden I knew what I had to say!

"The main reason I like it," I announced, "is because of the 'pling' at the very end."

"Much better," said James.

"It's only a trick with the guitar," I continued, "but it provides the record with a perfect signature. Moreover, I like the fact that the 'pling' is preserved in the groove for all eternity."

"Good."

I cast my eyes around the room and felt a powerful wave of energy surging through me.

"All these records look the same," I declared, "but they're all different. Different performers, different styles, different producers and different influences. There's a unique sound preserved in each and every groove, and that's why records are so important!"

The instant I ceased talking I felt the energy fading away. James was now peering at me intently.

"Good," he said again. "You've proved yourself thoroughly capable of making a confession."

"Amazing," I murmured.

"Quite."

"And I always thought I was a closed book."

"Apparently not."

"Mind you, I wouldn't want to do it too often," I said. "I'm exhausted."

James paused a moment before answering.

"So you've nothing else to confess then?" he asked.

I noticed he was still peering at me with the same intent expression.

"Of course not," I said, feeling mildly affronted by the remark. "I've told you everything."

"I see."

"You should get Keith to come here if you want to experiment," I added. "He'd be a much better candidate than me."

"I'll bear it in mind," said James.

He was still acting rather frostily, so I was relieved when he suggested we adjourn to the kitchen for a cup of tea.

"I suppose you've earned it," he said grudgingly.

Once he'd boiled the kettle and located the biscuit tin he began to ease up, but even then only slightly. I watched as he paced restlessly around the kitchen, opening cupboards and closing them again. In an attempt to lighten the atmosphere I tried to engage him in a bit of gossip.

"By the way," I said. "Talking of Keith, I meant to tell you he accidentally took home my 'Heroes and Villains' last night."

James stopped pacing around and turned to face me.

"Keith did?" he enquired.

"Yes," I said. "I ended up with 'Looking For Lewis and Clark'."

He took a deep breath.

"Dear oh dear," he said. "I wish you'd mentioned it earlier."

With that he strode out of the kitchen towards his music room, returning half a minute later with my copy of "Heroes and Villains".

"So presumably Keith's got your record?" I said.

"Presumably, yes."

"Do you know where he lives?"

"No."

"Nor me."

"Anyway, it's not mine: it's Alice's."

James appeared deeply troubled by the loss. Mislaying someone else's record was a serious misdemeanour and he would doubtless have to explain himself to Alice. Worse, he'd clearly suspected me of being involved in the "switch" and was probably now suffering a profound sense of guilt about it. For this reason, I decided not to pursue the matter.

"I'm sure it'll be perfectly safe with Keith until next Monday," I said.

"I hope you're right," said James.

Lurking in the back of my mind, however, was a picture of the mysterious record. It had held a fascination for me ever since I'd first laid eyes on the plain white label inscribed with the figures 4/25. I'd caught a glimpse of it once or twice since then, and on each occasion it became increasingly enticing. We'd come very close to hearing it the previous evening before George barged in on us, and then it had chanced to fall into Keith's hands. I wondered how long he'd resist the temptation to play it. After all, the next meeting was nearly a week away. It seemed a very long time to wait.

Meanwhile I pretended to be totally unaware of the secrecy surrounding the record. I asked James nothing about it, and likewise he told me nothing. Instead we began preparing for the following Monday. Our principal objective was to practise the art of listening without comment or judgement. Therefore we put the recent upheavals behind us and looked forward to a fruitful session of the Forensic Records Society. Unfortunately we hadn't bargained for our opponents' next move.

I walked into the Half Moon at ten to eight and saw Mike, Rupert, Chris and Dave sitting at the usual corner table. They were being besieged by a group of women all dressed in identical T-shirts bearing the words: I CONFESSED. Among them I recognised the tearful blonde woman from the other week. At that very moment she was homing in on Chris, urging him to join her and her companions in the Confessional Records Society. He wore a dazed expression and appeared nonplussed by the assault. Over at the bar I noticed Barry on his own, so I swiftly joined him. He'd just bought a round of drinks, but was in no particular hurry to return to the table.

"I'm waiting till they've gone," he said. "They've been here twenty minutes already."

"Must be having a recruitment drive," I remarked.

"Suppose so," said Barry. "What I can't understand is why they're so keen to enrol newcomers when they've already turned Keith and Mike away."

"It's not quite that simple," I said. "They're seeking people who are capable of making a proper confession. People who'll bare themselves to their cohorts. Keith and Mike failed to match these requirements."

Barry peered at me closely.

"Oh yes?" he said. "You seem to know a lot about the subject."

"Not really," I replied. "I've just done a little research, that's all."

"You're not thinking of joining them then?"

"Certainly not."

He continued peering at me for several seconds, and I thought I detected a hint of suspicion in his manner.

"Believe me," I said, "there's absolutely no question of my defecting to the CRS. Can you imagine me in one of those T-shirts? I don't think so. Apart from looking ridiculous, they're the trappings of a movement that's inherently weak. It's a complete sham. It has no proper foundations, so instead it reassures itself with a constant stream of new recruits. Hence all those women pestering Chris and the others. Yet even newcomers are weeded out if they don't fit the bill. The CRS aren't really interested in listening to records: they only want to tell other people about them. Keith and Mike were rejected out of hand, so what chance would I have? I'm a forensic man through and through."

"Well, I'll concede that," said Barry. "You definitely like listening to records."

"Thank you."

"Whether you like music," he added, "is a different matter entirely."

"What!" I said in dismay. "Who've you been talking to?"

"Nobody," he replied. "I reach my own conclusions."

I was about to demand what these conclusions were, exactly, when I noticed James emerge from the back room and gaze all around the pub. He appeared rather preoccupied and seemed oblivious to the women in the

T-shirts. Actually he looked as if he was searching for someone in particular, and I then realised that the only person missing was Keith. A glance at the clock told me it was now almost eight. James withdrew into the back room with a very worried expression on his face, so I decided to go through and offer what assistance I could.

The door was ajar as I approached, and before entering I happened to peek inside. The sight I beheld made me stop in my tracks. Alice was standing with her hands on her hips, glaring fiercely at James and speaking to him in a low, intense voice. For his part James stood meekly absorbing the flak. Alice was undoubtedly very cross, and while I was pleased to discover I wasn't the only person being given a hard time lately, the scene was nevertheless quite disturbing. Evidently both Alice and James were unaware of my presence, so I stealthily returned the way I'd come and waited for a couple of minutes. Very soon the others joined me and then we all entered the back room *en masse*. In that short interval everything had changed. Alice was now behind the bar polishing glasses and James sat staring nonchalantly at the red portable. I only hoped the ceasefire could be maintained for the duration of the meeting.

After formally noting Keith's absence, James allowed us a few seconds to prepare our selections.

"Right," he said. "It's Rupert's turn to begin, I think."

Rupert had chosen "Train to Skaville" as his first offering, but just as he handed it to James the door burst open and Keith walked into the room. He was clutching a record.

"You must forgive this interruption," he proclaimed, "but I have a confession to make."

It was obvious he was in a highly distressed condition.

"Come in and close the door," said James calmly. "You don't want anyone outside to hear, do you?"

"Oh," said Keith. "No, I suppose I don't."

He turned and pulled the door to, then walked over and placed the record on the table. It had a plain white label inscribed with the figures 4/25.

"Last week," he said, "in the flurry of departure I accidentally took this record home with me."

"Is that your confession?" said James.

"No," said Keith. "My confession is that I played it."

From somewhere behind the bar I heard a sigh of exasperation. Presumably James heard it too.

"Well," he said. "I must say I'm very surprised." His tone remained calm and measured. "After your experience the other week I'd have thought you'd know better than to play other people's records without permission. You said yourself you felt violated, and that was merely after someone looked through your collection. This is much worse."

"I'm sorry," murmured Keith in despair. "I tried to resist for several days, but eventually temptation got the better of me."

"A disappointing lapse."

"Marvellous record, though," Keith added. "It's . . ."

"Yes, that's enough, thank you," said James firmly. "Don't forget comments and judgements are forbidden."

"Sorry."

James paused to consider the case.

"Well, you do appear rather contrite about this," he said.

"Yes," replied Keith. "I am."

"Even so, you'll understand that some kind of penalty must be incurred."

"Yes."

There was a stunned silence all around the table.

"So if everyone's in full agreement I suggest a fortnight's suspension from the society."

The stunned silence persisted. I had no idea what the others were thinking, but I was so surprised by the severity of the punishment that I found myself at a complete loss for words. Furthermore, it seemed to me that although James was handing down the sentence, it was Alice who stood behind him urging retribution. Without doubt, her brooding presence had affected the final outcome.

"Agreed then," said James. "Alright, Keith, we'll see you in two weeks' time."

"Thank you," said Keith. He turned and headed for the door, and next moment he was gone.

"Isn't there a danger of driving him into the arms of the CRS?" I ventured.

"That's just a risk we'll have to take," James replied. "It'll be a good test of his commitment."

I was sure I'd heard James utter this remark before somewhere, and I had an uneasy feeling about it. Across the table I noticed Chris raising his eyebrows just as he'd done on many previous occasions, so perhaps he remembered it too. He voiced no opinion, however; and neither did Barry, who tended generally to be very outspoken on questions of form. Instead the meeting resumed as if the interruption had never taken place. The difference was that now there were only seven of us listening to each others' records, rather than eight, which struck me as a sorry state of affairs. It was always the same when sanctions were applied for the sake of some principle. Keith may have paid a heavy price for his misconduct, but the true cost fell on the rest of us.

As the session continued I began to reflect on my own position in the Forensic Records Society, and I soon decided I was scarcely better placed than Keith. Not only was I being constantly assailed by Alice, but now Barry had joined in the attack too. It all swung around the ludicrous allegation that I didn't really like music, a claim which could be neither proved nor disproved. I was no longer even certain if I could depend on James's support: his ongoing secrecy regarding the mysterious record suggested the opposite. It was still lying on the table where Keith had left it, and I'd been harbouring the thought that we might actually get to hear it sometime during the evening. This hope was abruptly dashed when Alice came around from behind the bar and took it away. She was wearing her usual platform shoes, and as she passed by

I again wondered how on earth she managed to walk in them. James probably knew the answer, but I could hardly ask him.

Chris was now on his second selection: he'd chosen "Days of Pearly Spencer". For the next few minutes we sat at the table in our various attitudes (serene, solemn, mesmerised and so forth) and the record seemed to capture the mood of the meeting. Despite the vast array of music on offer, the overriding tone had drifted gradually into melancholy. I was coming to regret my failure to defend Keith more robustly, and I was clearly not alone in this sentiment. He was our newest recruit, after all, and in hindsight I realised we'd treated him most shabbily.

The sense of betrayal deepened when we emerged from the back room at eleven o'clock and found Keith sitting on his own in the corner. On the table in front of him were three empty beer glasses. For some reason I'd assumed he'd go straight home after being suspended; instead he'd spent a solitary evening only a few yards away from us. This made the punishment seem even harsher. There was no sign of the women in the T-shirts, and it occurred to me that in his present state Keith would have been very easy prey for them. I was just considering whether I should go and console him when I was joined by Mike.

"I forgot to bring your record back," he said. "Alright to borrow it for another week?"

"Suppose so," I said. "A week's not very long, is it?"

"No," he replied, "but a fortnight is."

He didn't need to elaborate further: I could tell how he felt merely by the look on his face. Mike plainly shared my misgivings about the treatment meted out to Keith, and like me he'd failed abjectly to speak out on his behalf. We had to do something to redeem our shortcomings and in a few moments we reached a tacit agreement: together we would form a united front. A force for moderation. We were powerless to overturn the sentence, but at least we could offer Keith some moral support. Our resolve vanished just as quickly, however, when James and Alice suddenly appeared from the direction of the back room. James was carrying the red portable, and when he noticed Keith he gave him a curt nod of acknowledgement before descending into the cellar. Alice ignored Keith (and me) and went to help George close the main bar. It was now well past eleven and the Half Moon was emptying rapidly. In consequence we only had time to nod at Keith as we filed past him and headed into the darkness of the night.

When I got home I went straight to my turntable and played "Babylon is Burning" three times in succession; then I climbed into bed and lay dwelling on the situation we'd got ourselves into. Was it really beyond human capacity, I pondered, to create a society which didn't ultimately disintegrate through internal strife? Or collapse under the weight of its own laws? Or suffer damaging rivalries with other societies? Because there was no question that all these fates awaited us if we carried on as we were. The threat they posed loomed ever larger as I drifted off to sleep. They probably accounted for the peculiar dream I had just before dawn in which somebody was removing my records from their sleeves one by one and "skimming" them recklessly into oblivion. Amidst the chaos it was difficult to tell whether the culprit was James the Puritan, Alice the Accuser or Phillip the Confessor, or possibly a combination of all three, but I was thankful when daybreak came and I finally awoke.

In the cold light of a spring morning I saw the matter in a much clearer perspective. Immediately I realised that my concerns about Keith were completely out of proportion. For a start he'd already been examined and rejected by the CRS, so it was hard to imagine them trying to recruit him again. Furthermore, the diligence he'd applied after the episode with the long-players showed him to be a true forensics man. Recently he'd committed an indiscretion for which he'd paid dearly. Hence in the final analysis the sentence he'd received was essentially for his own good; I had little doubt that once he'd served it his standing in the society would improve by leaps and bounds. With these thoughts in mind I decided that all Keith needed to do was bide his time.

There was a crucial factor, however, which I hadn't allowed for. When I arrived at the Half Moon the following Monday I saw Mike, Dave, Barry, Chris and Rupert at the usual corner table. Sitting amongst them was Keith, and he was holding forth on a subject of apparent urgency. I bought a pint of Guinness before going over to join them.

"I just had to tell somebody," Keith was saying. "It's absolutely marvellous."

"Worth getting expelled for?" said Mike.

"Oh yes," replied Keith, "and anyway I was only suspended."

The exchange told me they were discussing the mysterious record, and all of a sudden I was overcome with jealousy. This was both irrational and foolish, but I was unable to suppress a sense of having missed out. Ever since I'd seen it lying on the turntable I'd felt I had some kind of stake in the record, although admittedly a minor one. I'd been convinced that sooner or later I'd be amongst the first to be let into the secret, yet now Keith had gone and stolen a march on me. He'd effectively moved above me in the pecking order, and I had no choice but to listen meekly with the others as he described what he'd heard.

"It's a girl with a guitar," he said. "Very basic, probably a demo, but also quite sophisticated."

"You mean like 'Drive Away My Heart'?" enquired Dave.

"Sort of," replied Keith, "but it's more unearthly. Almost ethereal actually."

"You mean like 'Song to the Siren'?" suggested Barry.

"Yes, but rather edgy too."

" 'White Rabbit'?"

"Not that edgy."

" 'Night Terror'?"

"Closer," said Keith, "but not as dark."

He was plainly struggling to find the appropriate words, and this only served to deepen my envy. I was certain that if I'd been in his place I could have expressed it much better. Unfortunately I wasn't.

"When you say it's a girl with a guitar," I asked, "do you mean a girl or a woman?"

"Well, a young woman I suppose," Keith answered.

"And what sort of guitar?"

"Acoustic, but interestingly enough I thought it could easily have been played on an electric and sound even better."

"So she could front a band, could she?" said Mike.

"Oh yes," declared Keith. "No question about it."

For some reason we all lapsed into silence, and as I looked at my companions I debated whether any of them had drawn the same conclusion as me. In my opinion it was obvious that the "girl" on the record was Alice, but I was unsure if the others had yet realised. If they had they didn't let on, so I resolved for the time being to keep it to myself. Besides, they were most likely preoccupied with the coming session. It was almost eight o'clock, so we gathered up our records and prepared to move. Keith remained all alone at the corner table, and when we headed for the back room I noticed some women in T-shirts eyeing him closely.

So began the eighth meeting of the Forensic Records Society. In the outside world spring had arrived and the days were getting longer, but all we were interested in was playing our selections to one another. First up was Rupert, who'd chosen "Here I Am Baby, Come and Take Me", and Dave followed with "Sock It to 'Em J.B.

Part One". We seemed set for a successful evening, and I was delighted when Barry's turn came around and he submitted "Happenings Ten Years Time Ago". This was another of my perennial favourites, and as we listened I sensed that I wasn't alone in my appreciation. Chris, for example, appeared to be paying particular attention to the record, and after the fade-out I wasn't surprised when he made one of his concise utterances:

" 'Pop group, are you?' " he said.

Those were his only words, but we all knew exactly what he meant. Well most of us did anyway. A small minority had a different interpretation, and this caused a rift which would have far-reaching consequences for the society.

"Sorry," said Barry, "but it's 'What group are you?' "

"No," replied Chris. "It's definitely 'pop group'."

"He's right," I added. " 'Pop group, are you?' "

"You're wrong," said Barry. "I've heard it a thousand times."

"So have I."

" 'What group are you?' " said Dave. "It makes sense."

"So does 'pop group'."

"Yes, but it's wrong."

"No, it isn't."

By this stage voices were being raised and hostile glances exchanged. Behind the corner bar I was aware of Alice regarding us all with mounting disdain, and as the bickering intensified she decided to intercede.

"Oh for goodness' sake!" she cried. "It hardly makes any difference, does it?"

In the shocked silence that ensued, James turned to Alice and addressed her directly.

"Actually it does make a difference," he said. "A great deal of difference."

Alice stared at him in astonishment.

"However," James continued, "this is neither the time nor the place for such disputes. Therefore, to avoid further disruption I propose an outright ban on quotations from records."

"Isn't that a bit stern?" I ventured.

"I'm afraid not," said James. "In fact it's my belief that we've been too tolerant for too long. The purpose of these meetings is to listen to records without comment or judgement. Anything else is a mere distraction."

"S'pose."

"So if everyone agrees, the ban can start immediately."

The shocked silence was yet to fade away, and with every second that ticked by James further tightened his grip on the Forensic Records Society.

"Agreed then," he said at length. "Whose turn is it next?"

"Mine," said Chris glumly.

I glanced at him and knew at once that he was wallowing in disgruntlement. Poor Chris! His moments of occasional glory had been snatched away without recompense, and I had to admit I felt rather sorry for him. Of course, James was perfectly correct in calling for a ban on quotations. All the same I lamented the passing of a quaint tradition, seemingly never to be revived.

It so happened that Chris had chosen "Love Will Tear Us Apart", a record which in normal circumstances would have provided plenty of quotable lines. Instead, when it ended he was obliged to observe a code of silence.

By all appearances the meeting continued much as it had before, and there was no obvious cause for concern. Just beneath the surface, though, was an underlying tension which broke through from time to time as we worked around the table. It was barely anything, scarcely perceptible, but when Mike selected "Six Months in a Leaky Boat" I began to sense that rebellion was afoot.

Maybe James sensed it too. Despite his recent consolidation of power he looked decidedly unsettled. Perhaps he was suffering the loneliness of leadership, or possibly he regretted contradicting Alice (a surefire recipe for trouble). Whatever the reason, he was plainly agitated about something. He was sitting opposite me, and as I watched him abstractedly shuffling his records I suddenly recognised one of the labels. It was plain white and bore the figures 4/25, which meant he was again in possession of the mysterious recording. We were now late into the evening and James had already played his first two choices, so I assumed he was saving it until last.

Meanwhile Dave and Barry had their final turns, and they each chose alternative versions of "I'm a Man".

"Just a coincidence," remarked Barry, but I wasn't so sure. From where I sat it looked like yet another case of insurgency.

The meeting was drawing to a close and only one selection remained unplayed. After a brief pause James removed the mysterious record from its sleeve and placed it on the deck. We all shared the feeling of excitement: finally we were going to hear it in the refined setting of the Forensic Records Society.

Our expectations were dashed, however, when Alice abruptly stalked around from behind the bar and seized the record.

"But I thought you agreed," James protested.

"Yes, well, I've changed my mind," said Alice. "It's quite obvious this lot aren't ready yet."

With that she turned and headed for the door, leaving us all staring at each other in disappointment. A minute or so later George appeared and began tidying up the corner bar.

"I've temporarily swapped jobs with Alice," he said, by way of explanation. "I'm not sure why."

There was nothing left to do except pack away our records. In those dying moments I remembered that Keith had spent the entire evening all alone, so as soon as I was ready I rushed out to see how he was. To my consternation I discovered him laughing and joking with the women in the T-shirts; and when I tried to catch his attention he looked right through me.

It was gone eleven and Alice was hard at work washing, polishing and stacking the empty glasses. There was no chance of obtaining a late drink from her, so I returned to the back room to try my luck with George. Sadly he wasn't in the mood for granting favours, which meant this option was closed as well.

Actually he'd almost finished tidying, and once he'd emptied the till his duties would be complete. He propped open the door with a broom, then deftly removed the till drawer and carried it away.

"Switch the lights out, will you?" he said over his shoulder. "I'll be locking up in ten minutes."

Barry and the others had already begun drifting homeward. The only person left in the room was James. He was sitting at the table gazing at the red portable, and didn't seem to notice me until I sat down opposite.

"What did Alice mean," I asked, "when she said we weren't ready yet?"

James regarded me for several moments before replying.

"You won't be offended?" he enquired.

"I'll try not to be."

"Well the truth is she thinks we're all emotionally retarded."

"What? You included?"

"I'm afraid so," said James, "though perhaps to a lesser extent than the rest of you."

"Oh."

"You've probably gathered she's a musician," he continued.

"Yes," I said. "Thought so."

"About a year ago she recorded a demo with this up-and-coming producer. It was a low-budget outfit and they only pressed twenty-five copies, most of which were sent off to the big record companies."

"How come nobody snapped her up then?"

"Good question," said James. "The trouble is, Alice is a very private person and doesn't like performing live. When the labels found out they lost interest and said no thank you."

"I see."

"It's made her very choosy about who hears the remaining copy."

"Is there only one?"

"Yep."

"But surely," I said, "this would be the ideal place to play it."

"Why?"

"Because we don't allow comments or judgements."

Surprisingly, James appeared unimpressed by the logic of my argument. He shook his head slowly and gave a long sigh before rising to his feet.

"It's not that simple," he said. "She thinks we're all emotionally retarded."

"Oh yes," I said. "Sorry, I forgot."

"I've been trying to persuade her for weeks and now she's gone and changed her mind again."

I realised I was ill-equipped to offer James advice on the subject, so I didn't pursue the conversation any further. It also struck me as the wrong time to tell him about Keith's encounter with the women in the T-shirts. This was probably the last news he wished to hear at present.

Nonetheless it was clear that we couldn't merely abandon Keith to his fate. There was no sign of him when I eventually left the Half Moon, and by the time I'd walked home I'd become deeply concerned about his welfare. Oh I was aware that his suspension only had another seven days to run, after which he could resume full participation in the Forensic Records Society. Yet tomorrow was Tuesday and the women from the CRS were summoned to their confession. What hope would Keith have if they tempted him to join them? None at all, I imagined, which was why I felt constrained once more to pay an unofficial visit.

The worst part of such a plan was the interminable waiting. I woke up next morning much earlier than usual having spent a restless night worrying in case James discovered what I was up to. As far as I knew the instruction to avoid the Half Moon on Tuesdays still stood, and I was taking a great risk going anywhere near the place. After careful reflection, however, I decided that James had his hands full dealing with Alice and was therefore unlikely to bother about me. Even so, there were many hours until evening and I found the time dragged heavily. I finally resorted to counting and playing all the records in my collection by women performers. The process took me most of the day, and the statistics were inconclusive. According to my research I owned sixty-eight records featuring women singing either solo or with a band, plus a large number of "mixed" ensembles. I wondered what Alice would make of these figures considering that, in her opinion, a) I didn't like music and b) I was emotionally retarded. Still, it helped pass the time.

In retrospect my efforts might have been better spent devising a sensible course of action. I'd given no proper thought to what I'd do if I bumped into Keith at the

Half Moon (or anyone else for that matter). Instead I blundered in totally unprepared.

I could tell straightaway that the Confessional Records Society was thriving. There were twice as many people in the pub as normal, mostly women, and many holding pink numbered tickets in readiness. I glanced around at the various groups and within moments my misgivings about Keith were confirmed. There he was, seated at our usual corner table surrounded by several of his new-found friends. Like them he held a pink numbered ticket, a fact that suggested I'd arrived too late to help him. Moreover, he seemed entirely oblivious to my presence. My attempts to attract his attention were all in vain, but I was reluctant to approach the table directly in case the women in T-shirts tried to convert me as well. Instead I searched for a place near the bar, from where I could keep an eye on the comings and goings. Which was when I noticed James. He was sitting on the stool I'd occupied during my previous foray, and was apparently watching my every move. I gave him a nod and he beckoned me to join him.

"Good evening," he said. "I've been expecting you."

"Really," I answered. "Why's that then?"

"Well, let's say it's becoming a bit of a habit of yours," he replied. "By my reckoning this is at least your second visit."

"You're very well-informed," I said. "I suppose Alice reported me, did she?"

"She mentioned it, yes."

"So you decided to intercept me."

"No, no," said James. "As a matter of fact I think we're both here for the same reason."

"You mean Keith?"

"Yes."

"So you don't suspect me of being a confessor?"

"Of course not."

It transpired that James had anticipated my arrival and there was a pint of Guinness waiting for me in the pump. The revelation made me feel rather guilty because I'd been on the verge of demanding exactly what gave him the right to break his own rules. After all, he'd forbidden the entire Forensic Records Society from attending the Half Moon on Tuesdays; yet here he was sitting as bold as brass in the heart of the rival encampment. His explanation was simple. He told me that Alice had kept him notified about the women in the T-shirts; and that he'd become particularly alarmed about their manoeuvres where Keith was concerned. Accordingly he'd chosen to set his personal reservations aside and attend the CRS as a strictly neutral observer. He'd made a calculated guess that I would do the same, which would hopefully provide safety in numbers.

"Well you might have told me," I chided.

"Yes," he said, "and so might you."

A temporary lull in the general hubbub allowed us to hear the faint music which was drifting from the direction of the back room.

"Sounds like 'Goodbye Yellow Brick Road'," said James.

"Yes," I agreed.

For the next couple of minutes we strained to listen until the record reached its dramatic conclusion. This was followed by a pregnant pause, then we watched as the door opened and a woman plunged into the tearful embraces of her companions. She was plainly overcome by the experience, but she was in good hands. No sooner had they swept her away than Phillip emerged and cast his gaze over the assembly.

"Who's next?" he enquired.

"Me," said Keith. "Number seventeen."

I thought I saw Phillip regarding him a little curiously as he approached, but he said nothing and led him into the back room. We listened carefully and after a few moments a disembodied voice floated into our hearing.

"'It's awfully considerate of you to think of me here'," it sang, "'and I'm most obliged to you for making it clear that I'm not here'."

I knew the record immediately.

"Good choice, Keith," I murmured.

To my surprise I received a sharp reprimand from James. He spoke quietly but firmly.

"We mustn't let our standards slip," he said, "especially in these surroundings."

"How do you mean?" I asked.

"We should always adhere to our doctrine," he replied. "No comments or judgements."

"Oh yes," I said. "Sorry."

I redoubled my efforts and concentrated hard. The voice in the back room was gradually being overtaken by a demented brass band that threatened to drag it into obscurity. Next came a psychedelic interlude, after which the voice made a slight return. All of a sudden the song ended. There was a brief hiatus, then the door opened and Keith was gently but persuasively ejected. He was carrying a long-playing record and looked decidedly pale.

"Keith!" I called, but he paid me no attention and headed rapidly through the seething throng towards the exit. I made to go after him, only to feel a restraining hand on my arm. It belonged to James.

"Let him go," he said. "He'll be better off away from here."

"But I thought we were meant to take care of him," I protested. "He's had quite a rough time lately."

"I know," said James, "but he needed to learn his lesson. This episode should ensure his safe return to the fold."

Just then the crowd began to stir, and seconds later Phillip reappeared in the doorway.

"Number eighteen?" he enquired.

We watched as he scanned the room for the next candidate, and inevitably his gaze fell on the pair of us. I could tell he recognised me at once, but I was uncertain if he knew who James was. Even so, the gaze swiftly transformed into a stare.

"Here I am!" called a woman with a pink ticket. "Number eighteen!"

She approached Phillip tentatively, but he ignored her and continued staring at James. For his part, James returned the stare with equal intensity. A few moments passed and then Phillip came over to us. He and James were now only a yard apart, each eyeing the other so acutely that my palms had gone sticky.

"How about you?" said Phillip.

"I think not," James replied.

"Nothing to confess then?"

"Not in your hearing."

"I see."

Phillip paused to absorb the full import of James's denial.

"Do you believe in confession?" he asked at length.

"No," said James.

"And you don't allow comments or judgements?"

"Correct."

"A very narrow path."

"From which we will not stray."

"So I gather."

Without a further word Phillip turned and marched into the back room. Shortly afterwards his two accomplices emerged and ushered the bewildered woman inside. Proceedings then resumed behind closed doors.

While all this was happening a hush had descended over the startled onlookers. Whether any of them understood the significance of the confrontation was unclear, but I detected a wave of relief as the silence faded and normality was restored. James, in the meantime, remained totally unperturbed.

"That man must have spies everywhere," he remarked. "Like another pint?"

"Actually, it's my round next," I said. "Where's George got to?"

106

"Not sure," said James. "He seems to have vanished."

There was no sign of the landlord for several minutes, but eventually he came striding up the steps from the cellar wearing a very smart (though rather old-fashioned) three-piece suit.

"Can either of you tell the difference between red and white wine?" he asked.

"Of course," replied James.

"Good," said George. "You can man the bar while I have my free confession."

"How do you mean 'free'?" I queried.

"Well, it's usually five pounds a go."

"What!" I said. "Since when?"

"He started charging last week," George explained. "Not me, though. I get mine in lieu of rent."

"Number nineteen!" called a voice from the doorway.

Phillip's assistants had reappeared and stood waiting for George to join them. After he'd gone James moved into position behind the bar, and I helped out by collecting empty glasses. After a few seconds we heard music coming from the back room. George had chosen "Islands in the Stream", and as it played I pondered the latest piece of news.

So Phillip was now charging a fee for each confession! Presumably Keith had refused to pay and this was the reason he'd been rejected. Nevertheless there were plainly scores of others who were willing to part with their hard-earned money so that a comparative stranger could peer into their inner selves. The very idea of it made me squirm with distaste, and

I was baffled by George's apparent eagerness to participate. I'd have thought a hard-headed business-man like him would have been more sceptical. Admittedly he'd avoided paying the fee, yet he'd gone to the trouble of changing into a suit before his confession was heard! I could only surmise that beneath the bluff exterior lay a sentimental soul.

"Islands in the Stream" duly ended and George emerged from the back room trying desperately to restrain his tears. He received a round of applause from the assembled women, then came behind the bar and dismissed James and me from our duties.

"Thanks for the help," he said. "You can have a pint each on the house."

Such generosity was practically unknown in the Half Moon, and I debated whether George had somehow been altered by his recent experience. A little later, however, he abruptly quashed the notion.

"By the way," he announced. "Your free trial period expires at the end of the month."

"Oh yes?" said James.

"If you wish to keep the back room after that you'll have to pay me some rent."

"But you weren't using it until we came along," I objected.

"True," said George, "but there's been a sudden upsurge in demand."

"Really?"

"I'm receiving a constant stream of enquiries."

Faced with these facts we had no alternative but to accede to George's ultimatum. We quickly agreed terms, then James and I retired to a corner to discuss the situation.

"Rather unfortunate," said James. "It means we'll have to start charging for membership."

"But won't that make us as bad as the CRS?" I asked.

"Not really," he replied. "We're merely covering a running cost, whereas they profit from each confession."

"Bunch of charlatans."

"Indeed."

Having established that ours was the more righteous cause, we decided that there was nothing to be gained from staying any longer. We finished our pints and made plans for the following Monday.

"I'll send round a memo," said James, "informing the others about the membership fee."

"Good thinking," I said. "Then they can come prepared."

As soon as I got home that night I went straight to my turntable and played "Every Day Should Be a Holiday" three times in succession; then I climbed into bed and considered the latest turn of events. The stand-off with Phillip had demonstrated once and for all that the Forensic Records Society would never be reconciled with the CRS. All the same, I felt we were under much less pressure than before. Our resolve in the face of overwhelming opposition had proved we had the strength to continue on our present course. Any previous doubts had been removed. We had no need to make confessions about our records; for us it sufficed simply to listen without comment or judgement. The only problem was the projected membership fee, but this was a trifling matter which I was certain could be easily overcome.

Regrettably my optimism was short-lived. I arrived on the appointed evening to discover there were only six of us in attendance. Chris and Keith were nowhere to be seen, and James insisted on beginning punctually at eight.

"Latecomers will not be admitted," he declared.

As it transpired, there were no latecomers. The session went as well as might be expected under the circumstances, but none of us could ignore the prospect of our numbers dwindling further still. The gloom deepened when we emerged from the back room at half past ten. During the meeting a new poster had appeared on the wall next to ours:

PERCEPTIVE RECORDS SOCIETY
MEETS EVERY WEDNESDAY
9PM
HALF MOON
BRING SOME RECORDS AND SHARE YOUR
PERCEPTIONS

Whoever designed the poster had gone to a great deal of trouble over its style and content. They'd employed pastel colours with flowery decorations and a contrasting border, and it put the neighbouring posters to shame. When we read it we reached a variety of conclusions.

110

"Obviously a splinter group," said James. "Most probably Chris and Keith protesting about the new fees."

"Doesn't it run a bit deeper than that?" I ventured. "After all, they've been very careful with their presentation."

"Perceptive Records," said Dave. "It certainly chimes in with Keith's preference for long-players."

"Oh I think Chris is the driving force," said Barry. "I expect he wants to exercise his right to quote."

Whatever the reason, a new society had been formed on our very doorstep and we had to decide how to react. Naturally James wanted to adopt a hard line with the renegades.

"We've given them chance after chance," he said, "and they've thrown it all back at us."

"So what do you suggest?" asked Dave.

"Permanent expulsion," James replied. "Anything less will only encourage others to join them."

"Steady on," I said. "If we keep expelling people we risk signing our own death warrant."

"Besides," said Barry, "you can't expel anybody."

"Why?" said James.

He seemed genuinely perplexed by the assertion.

"Because we're all equal members," Barry answered. "I disagree with Chris and Keith on several counts, but actually they're well within their rights."

"To set up a rival society?" demanded James.

"No," said Barry. "A society with different aims to ours."

"If they're sharing perceptions," Dave added, "surely they pose more of a threat to the confessionals than us."

"I think they sound quite harmless," said Mike.

"Harmless or not," said James, "they've betrayed us and should be punished accordingly."

James had patently failed to grasp that his own strict approach formed a large part of the problem. Moreover, it struck me as foolhardy to condemn people without trial. As the debate continued I went to the bar and consulted with George; he confirmed that Chris and Keith had been in the pub earlier and negotiated hiring the back room on Wednesday evenings. So now we knew for certain. I joined the others and related the news; then, after further discourse, Dave proposed a compromise.

"Instead of expelling or suspending anyone," he said, "why don't we send an envoy to the Perceptive Records Society?"

"For what purpose?" enquired James.

"Simply to maintain contact," said Dave. "You never know: we might even gain from allowing them a bit of freedom. Once they've let off steam they'll most likely return to the straight and narrow."

Dave's wise counsel finally won James over. The next step was to choose a suitable envoy.

"Definitely not me," said Barry. "I'm bound to clash with Chris over some obscure wording."

"Nor me," said Dave. "I'm against long-players."

For reasons of their own Mike and Rupert similarly ruled themselves out. Needless to say James couldn't possibly fill the role, and I gradually realised the mantle was about to fall on my shoulders.

"Alright, I'll volunteer," I said. "Should be interesting actually."

Annoyingly, I then had to endure a barrage of suggestions about the records I should take with me.

"What about 'Novocaine for the Soul'?" said Barry.

"Or 'Cool Meditation'," offered Dave.

"'Love is the Law'," urged Mike. "Three minutes forty-two seconds."

"Yes, well," I said, "I think you're all making misplaced assumptions about which direction they'll be moving."

"Only trying to help," said Mike.

"I know you are," I replied, "but if I'm to represent us properly I need a degree of independence."

As a matter of fact I found all their suggestions useful in the sense that I knew they were all wrong. The challenge I'd accepted was formidable because the Perceptive Records Society had introduced a new dimension to the art of listening. Therefore to gain their trust I needed to be highly assiduous in my choice of record. I had to convince them of my worth; otherwise they might brand me an impostor and kick me out.

"Oh, one last thing," I said. "I presume our door is always open if they ever want to come back?"

"Suppose so," said James with reluctance.

"Good," I remarked. "It'll be handy to have a trump card up my sleeve."

I looked at the clock and noticed it was getting rather late, then a movement in the doorway caught my eye.

113

Throughout the evening Alice had kept such a low profile that I'd almost forgotten she was there. She'd been operating the corner bar as usual, having apparently made her peace with James (I wasn't sure about the rest of us), and now she emerged from the back room carrying the red portable.

"You forgot this," she announced.

"Oh yes," said James. "Sorry."

He went swiftly over and took it from her, then carried it down into the cellar. Meanwhile George gave the bell its final ring.

"Come on, you lot," he bawled. "Out!"

It was time to leave, so the others wished me luck and I set off home. As I walked the dark streets I pondered what to take to the Perceptive Records Society. Many contenders sprang to mind, of course, arising from a very broad spectrum, and once again I realised the enormity of the task. How, for example, could I make a choice between "Sloop John B" and "Johnny B. Goode"; or between "Friday on my Mind" and "Friday I'm in Love"[1]; or between "Last Train to Clarksville" and "Magic Bus"? It was impossible, and by the time I reached home my head was spinning. Feeling tired and overwrought, I slumped on my bed and asked myself what on earth I'd let myself in for.

Only when I was on the verge of sleep did the answer arrive. It was like a light coming on, and suddenly I knew precisely which record to take.

---

[1] No easy choice for Robinson Crusoe

At ten o'clock the following morning I paid James an unscheduled visit. I had a long wait before he opened the door.

"Ah," he said, when he saw me.

"Hello," I replied. "Just dropped by on the off-chance."

"Er . . . right," he said. "Go through to the music room and I'll join you shortly."

Obviously the kitchen was still out of bounds, so I did as I was instructed and spent the next few minutes gazing around James's sanctuary. It was slightly less orderly than usual and several of his storage boxes had been lifted down from the shelves. This told me he'd been seeking particular records. Lying on his turntable was a copy of "(I Can't Get No) Satisfaction", but there were no other clues.

Eventually James appeared carrying a tray laden with tea and biscuits.

"Cinnamon Snaps," he said, as he handed me a cup and saucer. "I've run out of Malted Milks."

"That's odd," I said. "I thought you only got them in for me."

"I do normally," he said, "but somebody else likes them too."

It was tempting to ask who he meant, but I managed to resist (I could hazard a guess anyway). Instead, I changed the subject and nodded towards the deck.

"I see you've been giving the immortal rockers a spin."

"Yes," James answered. "It's part of a little side-project I've been engaged with."

"Really?"

"I'm playing all my records with bracketed titles."

"Don't tell me," I said. "'Keep Searchin' (We'll Follow the Sun)'?"

"Correct," said James.

"'(If Paradise Was) Half as Nice'?"

"Yep."

"'What Does It Take (to Win Your Love)'?"

"Good question."

"Don't forget '(S.O.S.)' and '(007)'."

"No," said James. "I won't."

I could have reeled off some more examples, but I sensed I'd gone far enough already.

"Sounds like an absorbing pastime," I remarked.

James switched on the deck and we listened to "Satisfaction" three times in a row. Afterwards we sat silently drinking our tea.

"Was there something you wanted to ask me?" he enquired at length.

"Actually," I said, "I was wondering if you could lend me a record."

"Certainly," he replied. "What do you want to borrow?"

Now I should mention here that, although James and I favoured the seven inch format, we each possessed a dozen or so long-players. We'd acquired them for various reasons over the years, and I happened to know James owned the one I had in mind. When I told him the title he was intrigued.

"Interesting selection," he observed. "Any specific reason?"

"Yes," I said, "and I'm afraid you might object."

"Why?"

"Because I want to take it to the Perceptive Records Society."

"I see."

I could tell from his expression that James was shocked by the request. He could easily have turned me down flat, but to his credit he allowed me to explain my motives before reaching a decision.

"I know you disapprove of them," I began, "and I admit we've suffered a split as a consequence of their actions. Nonetheless our ultimate purpose is to engineer their return to the fold, and therefore we should come bearing gifts."

"You mean give them my record?" said James with indignation.

"No, no, of course not," I said quickly. "That was merely a figure of speech."

"What then?"

"Well," I said, "as far as I can see they wish to broaden their perceptions."

"Yes."

"So this record pursues the idea to its logical conclusion."

James considered my words for a few moments.

"Don't you think you're perhaps being a bit too 'clever'?" he suggested.

"Maybe," I said, "but I'm hoping they'll be flattered by our efforts to please them."

"And then I'll get my record back?"

"Naturally."

The alternative was to let Keith and Chris go their own way with an entirely separate society, and I suspected James didn't really want that. He deliberated long and hard, then finally relented.

"Alright," he said, "you can give it a try."

"Thanks."

We celebrated the agreement by listening to "Satisfaction" once more for luck, and after it finished I recalled some other bracketed song titles:

"'Quick Joey Small (Run Joey Run)'."

"Oh yes," said James. "I'd forgotten about that."

"'(Your Love Keeps Lifting Me) Higher and Higher'."

"Yes."

"And lastly," I said, "'I'm the Leader of the Gang (I Am!)'."

"Definitely not included!" retorted James. "We don't mention him these days."

"No, I suppose not."

He paused expectantly.

"Can you think of any more?" he enquired.

"No."

James grinned with triumph, then went to one of this boxes and retrieved a record with a yellow and green label.

"Aha," I said. "Something progressive."

"In its day, yes."

He removed "Satisfaction" from the deck and substituted "Momma's Reward (Keep Them Freaks A-Rollin')".

"Isn't that a B-side?" I asked.

"Correct," James answered, "but it still counts."

We played the record three times in succession, as was our custom, then I decided I ought to get going. James showed me into the hallway.

"Best wishes for tonight's meeting," he said. "Let me know how you get on."

"Alright," I replied. At the same instant a belated thought occurred to me. "It's a shame I can't take Alice's record to play them."

"How do you mean?"

"Well," I said, "it would be a good test of their perceptions."

"But you've never heard it," said James. He glanced towards the kitchen door, which was closed. "Or have you?"

"No, I haven't," I said, "but Keith has and he was extremely impressed."

"Really?"

"Furthermore, he's passed the word to the rest of the society."

"Oh," said James. "I didn't know."

I left him contemplating this piece of information and headed homeward. With me I carried my passport to the Perceptive Records Society: namely, the long-player I'd procured from James. Quite a lot would depend on the outcome of my visit, so I decided to make careful preparations. This involved a scrupulous study of the sleeve notes (which were printed in English, French, German and Italian) as well as a trial run in the controlled environment of my own bedroom.

Once I'd played it through a couple of times I was convinced I'd made an inspired choice.

When evening came I sallied forth to the Half Moon, where it transpired that Keith and Chris had been making elaborate preparations of their own. Somehow they'd persuaded George to allow them to install a fifty-watt quadrophonic sound system in the back room.

"How did you manage that?" I asked with incredulity. "George has an aversion to loud noise."

"Bribery and corruption," said Keith. "It never fails."

Maybe so, but they hadn't attracted a single applicant for their nascent society. They sat waiting hopefully as the time ticked around to nine o'clock, then they accepted the inevitable and the meeting began.

"Glad you could come," said Chris. "Obviously we bear no ill feelings towards the forensics."

"Pleased to hear it," I replied.

"We simply needed more room to develop."

"So I gather."

Keith was peering with interest at my record.

"Are long-players admissible?" I enquired.

"Certainly," he said. "As a matter of fact anything goes."

"A commendable policy."

"And as our guest you're entitled to go first."

"Thanks."

The hi-fi belonged to Keith, but fortunately he wasn't one of those people who were "precious" about their equipment. He assumed I was competent to operate it safely, and watched in silence as I started the turntable and lowered the needle into the groove.

"'Music has dreamt far too long,'" I proclaimed. "'Now we shall awake'."

At that moment the door opened and a man looked in. The introductory bars of my chosen record had just begun, so I put my finger to my lips and beckoned him to come inside. He found a seat and nodded with approval at the turntable; clearly he recognised the series of chords that were gradually building up and filling the room. The composition was now reaching the first of its multiple crescendos. As we sat around the table in our various attitudes (serene, solemn, mesmerised and so forth) I realised the newcomer had arrived empty-handed. Still, he seemed content enough and appeared to be following the music closely. It was a long haul, but he waited until it had completely finished before speaking.

"*Also Sprach Zarathustra*," he said. "My name's Kevin, by the way."

Chris and Keith introduced themselves while I lifted the record from the deck and replaced it in its sleeve. At this point I thought perhaps there might be some kind of discussion before we moved on, but there was none. Plainly the old traditions continued to hold sway.

"So who's next?" said Keith. "How about you, Kevin?"

"Next with what?"

"A record."

Kevin was now starting to look slightly baffled.

"This is the film quiz, isn't it?" he asked.

"No," said Keith. "It's the Perceptive Records Society."

"You want the other Half Moon," added Chris.

"Where's that then?"

"Go down to the end of the road here, turn left, then third right and it's on your right."

"My mistake," said Kevin. "I've come to the wrong place." He stood up and walked solemnly to the door.

"Leave it open, will you?" said Chris.

Kevin turned to face us.

"I'm sorry, Dave," he said. "I'm afraid I can't allow that."

"Dave's not here," said Keith, but his words went unheeded. In an instant Kevin had gone.

If Chris and Keith were disappointed at this early loss, they didn't show it. Chris merely raised his eyebrows (his normal method of expression) while Keith removed another long-player from its sleeve. His opening selection was "Set the Controls for the Heart of the Sun", and as we sat listening I slowly drained my pint of Guinness. When the record ended there was a respectful silence. No comments or judgements; only perceptions, and these remained unvoiced.

"Anybody like another pint before we resume?" I asked.

The pair of them gladly accepted my offer, so I took the empty glasses and headed out into the main bar. Which was when I received an unpleasant surprise. I emerged from the back room to see a group of three men sitting at our usual corner table. I knew them at once: it was Phillip and the two Andrews from the

122

Confessional Records Society. Needless to say I pretended not to notice them and proceeded to place my order as normal. There was no doubt in my mind, however, that they were here to observe the comings and goings of the Perceptive Records Society; possibly even to intimidate would-be members with their presence. Moreover, it was quite probable they'd heard about the recent schism we'd suffered and were seizing the chance to gloat.

Well, I was determined to deny them the satisfaction!

I bought three pints from George and sauntered into the back room without giving the confessionals so much as a glance. At the same time, though, I decided not to say anything to Chris and Keith. I was trying to pursue a strategy of softly-softly; I didn't want it derailed by external forces.

They were patiently awaiting my return, and the next record was already cued up on the deck. It was "I Am the Walrus", and just before it began Chris quoted the line about Edgar Allen Poe.

This was the first time I'd heard Chris quote from a song prior to it even being played, and he was evidently enjoying his newly gained freedom. Nevertheless I couldn't help feeling that he and Keith were squandering the wider opportunities which were now open to them. I thought we were supposed to be breaking through the doors of perception, but actually the two of them didn't seem to know where to start.

Come to that, neither did I. My opening gambit with *Also Sprach Zarathustra* had been close to perfect; yet beyond that I, too, was out of my depth. All of a sudden the doctrine of the Forensic Records Society appeared not as a straitjacket but as a life raft. We listened to "I Am the Walrus", and afterwards there were no comments or judgements (or even quotations).

Even so, it would obviously be a while before Chris and Keith realised exactly what they'd forsaken. For the present they continued to labour under the delusion that they were somehow more perceptive than the rest of us. So it was that we heard "Deluxe Men in Space", "I Wanna Be Adored", "2000 Light Years from Home" and "She Sells Sanctuary" amongst others. The final contribution of the evening was "Give Peace a Chance"[1].

"'OK, beautiful,'" said Chris, as we wrapped up the session.

We adjourned to the main bar for a last drink, and I was glad to see that there was no longer any sign of the confessionals. Presumably they'd completed their observations and departed.

"Coming next Wednesday?" Keith asked.

"Sure," I replied. "You coming next Monday?"

"Time will tell," he said.

"Meaning what?"

"Meaning we'll think about it," said Chris.

This struck me as a rather one-sided bargain, but it was too late to withdraw from my commitment without losing face. I would simply have to stick to my plan and hope for the best. Besides, it wasn't as if attending the Perceptive Records Society had been any sort of

---

[1] Chorus repeated twenty times

hardship. To tell the truth I'd quite enjoyed myself, and I was interested to discover what unfolded at the next meeting.

A little later George called me over for a quiet word.

"Phillip and his friends were here earlier," he said.

"Yes," I said. "I noticed."

"They enquired about renting the back room on Mondays."

"But that's our night!"

"I know," said George. "I told them we had a prior agreement, and then they offered to outbid you. They were quite insistent actually. For some reason they seem dissatisfied with Tuesdays."

"I can't see what they've got to worry about," I said. "They appear to be doing very nicely, thank you very much."

George leaned in closer and lowered his voice.

"Why don't you start taking confessions yourselves?" he asked. "Then you could rake in a bit of extra cash on the side."

"We're not really like that," I explained. "It goes against our beliefs."

"Oh," said George, furrowing his brow. "Does it?"

He clearly didn't have the faintest understanding of the difference between the various societies which operated beneath his roof. The last thing I wanted to do, however, was fall out with our host. Therefore, I politely declined his suggestion and returned to join my companions. All the same I was deeply troubled by the news he'd imparted. Once again the arch-confessional had made a hostile move against the Forensic Records

Society, this time in a blatant attempt to supplant us from the popular Monday-evening slot. Fortunately Chris and Keith had no inkling of the narrowly averted crisis; otherwise their hand would have been strengthened considerably. I decided the situation was too delicate to press them on their future intentions, so I carefully avoided the subject. Instead we had a discussion about records which began with "Hey!"

The following morning I called on James to return his long-player. I arrived at ten o'clock and after a brief delay Alice opened the door.

"Oh," she said. "It's you."

"Yes," I replied. "James in?"

"No, he's gone out for a while."

"It's just that I've brought his record back."

"Oh yes?"

"And I also wanted to let him know how I got on last night."

"Well," she said, "I suppose you'd better come in."

As she led me inside I noticed she looked much slighter than usual; then I realised she'd discarded her towering platform shoes and was walking around barefoot. She paused outside the music room.

"You can entertain yourself in here till James comes back," she announced.

"How do you mean?" I enquired.

"Play a few records."

"Oh no," I said. "I couldn't do that."

"Why?"

"Not without permission."

"But I thought you were friends."

126

"We are," I said, "but it's simply not done."

Alice regarded me curiously.

"Very well," she said at length. "You can sit staring out of the window instead."

She showed me into the room and as I entered I glanced instinctively towards the record player. Lying on the turntable was a copy of "Don't Think Twice, It's All Right".

"'When your rooster crows at the break of dawn,'" I remarked, "'look out your window and I'll be gone.'"

Alice turned in the doorway.

"How do you know those words?" she asked.

"I just do."

"So you've heard it before?"

"Of course," I said. "I've got a copy at home."

"But normally you only like records with gimmicky bits."

"Not necessarily," I countered. "I like all sorts."

Alice peered at me reflectively.

"Oh," she said. "Maybe you're not as . . ."

I never found out what she was going to say next because suddenly the doorbell rang and she hurried off to answer it. A few moments later I heard voices in the hallway. James was back from his errand,[1] and when he came into the music room he looked as if he'd seen a ghost.

"It's worse than that," he explained, after he'd recovered a little. "I've just come past the Public

---

[1] He'd forgotten his key

Meeting Hall and there's a huge poster of Phillip on the billboard."

"Blimey," I said.

"Apparently they're planning to hold mass confessions down there on Thursday evenings."

James was evidently quite distraught. He was holding a packet of Malted Milk biscuits, but he seemed totally unaware of the fact until Alice gently removed them from his grasp.

"I'll go and make some tea," she said.

James gazed vacantly at the biscuits.

"Oh," he said. "Yes. Thanks."

"Could have been worse," I ventured, after she'd gone. "George told me they were trying to take over the back room on Mondays."

I went on to recount the events of the previous evening, and urged James that it was imperative to win Keith and Chris back to our cause. Without their support we'd be helpless against a mass movement.

"There's no doubt about it," I said. "Phillip is determined to suppress the Forensic Records Society by fair means or foul."

James pondered the situation.

"Phillip and his friends are obviously playing a numbers game," he said. "We know from our own experience that they tend to reject unsuitable candidates willy-nilly. On the other hand they need to maintain a constant flow of revenue. Presumably they've decided to make up the shortfall by adopting industrial methods."

"A scattergun approach," I suggested.

"Correct."

"With no hope for those who fall by the wayside."

As though to confirm our faith in the forensic principle, James went to the turntable and played "Don't Think Twice, It's All Right". While we were listening Alice came in with a trayful of tea and biscuits, and I thought she looked at me slightly less severely when she passed me my cup and saucer. I knew full well, however, that I should not take anything for granted. Therefore I made a mental note to choose my words carefully if and when we discussed music.

In the meantime, the remaining members of the Forensic Records Society had no alternative but to continue to plough our own furrow. I can't deny that I was rather disappointed the following Monday when Keith and Chris were absent once again, but I was pleased to note that most of the others had a positive outlook. Dave and Barry were without doubt the most firmly embedded of the rank and file; and Rupert, although he seldom spoke, showed no sign of wavering. The only cause for concern was Mike. Even after attending for several weeks he still displayed a periodic lack of confidence in his choice of records. This evening, for example, he'd plainly brought more than the specified number. He sat at the table slowly shuffling them as if unable to decide what to present to the rest of us. Amongst them, to his credit, was my copy of "Another Girl, Another Planet", which he duly returned to me. All the same, there were at least six records stacked in front of him when the session began.

Despite the reduced attendance the meeting proceeded more or less as usual. Alice was on duty behind the corner bar, and James presided over the red portable. I'd been worried that this might sound puny in comparison with the fifty-watt system employed by the Perspective Records Society. Very soon, though, my qualms were laid to rest. Dave's first choice of the evening was "Bad Moon Rising", a recording perfectly suited to the mono format.

"Right, let's get started," said James, "and remember: no comments, judgements or quotations."

He delivered the words in his normal uncompromising manner. We'd heard them on countless previous occasions, but tonight for some reason they produced a reaction from Mike. It was hardly anything, barely discernible, but nonetheless I could tell that some kind of watershed had been reached. Lying at the top of Mike's stack was a copy of "No Particular Place to Go", another record very much in the mono tradition. A moment earlier he'd seemed ready to present it as his opening contribution; now, however, he changed his mind and discreetly moved it out of sight. For the next two minutes seventeen seconds we sat around the table in our various attitudes (serene, solemn, mesmerised and so forth) and listened to "Bad Moon Rising". I only hoped it wasn't an omen of what lay ahead.

Fortunately, Rupert lightened the tone with "Israelites", then Barry followed with "Me and Baby Brother" (both sounding surprisingly mellow on the red portable). By the time we got to Mike's turn he'd settled for "Monkeys on Juice" and appeared wholly satisfied with his selection.

130

The final offering was "Are 'Friends' Electric?" (chosen by James) and while it was playing it struck me as a befitting contender for the Perceptive Records Society. In the same instant I realised I must learn to erase such thoughts from my conscience; otherwise I could end up on the same slippery slope as Chris and Keith. I reminded myself that my link with the PRS was strictly ambassadorial. My role was to investigate them and report back, whilst taking care not to fall under their influence. Even so it was clear that I needed to cultivate their favour, which in turn required me to take a set of worthy records to their meetings. Yet how could I make choices except by engaging my perceptions? I was still debating this quandary when the session ended and we drifted out into the main bar.

As soon as I emerged George beckoned me over.

"Phillip was here half an hour ago," he said. "He came to cancel his Tuesday evening booking."

"Oh, really?" I replied. "That's great news."

"What do you mean great?" George demanded. "It's a catastrophe!"

He was highly displeased, and when I considered the matter from his standpoint I could understand why. The Confessional Records Society had certainly generated large profits for the Half Moon and its passing would doubtless cause George a sleepless night or two. Still, it was only with some effort that I managed to express a degree of sympathy. In truth I was delighted that Phillip had decided to move on, and I couldn't wait to tell the others.

I glanced across at the corner table where Barry, Dave, Rupert and Mike had already congregated. They sat with their heads together and spoke to one another in urgent whispers. All of a sudden Mike shook his head sharply; then without a further word he rose to his feet and headed directly for the exit. The other three watched him go before calmly resuming their discussion.

"What was all that about?" enquired George.

"I don't know," I said. "I'm a bit of an outsider these days."

It was a fact I'd only just become aware of, yet when I thought about it properly I realised there'd been many signs and indications recently. Dave, Barry and Rupert evidently viewed themselves as the core group within the Forensic Records Society. Where Mike stood in the arrangement was difficult to tell, but I suspected there was some aspect he was unhappy about. All I knew was that they no longer sought my opinion; neither was I party to any of their conversations. Therefore I decided to keep the news about Phillip to myself.

James was equally isolated, of course, but in an entirely different way. When he and Alice eventually reappeared from the back room they paid no attention to anybody else and, after returning the red portable to the cellar, sat down at a separate table. It was gradually dawning on me that my days of sharing pints of Guinness with James were well and truly over.

When Tuesday evening came I was tempted to call in on the Half Moon to see for myself that the Confessional Records Society had indeed departed.

However, I swiftly changed my mind when I pictured George standing forlorn and abandoned behind his bar. Instead I began making preparations for Wednesday.

My previous foray to the Perceptive Records Society had been a partial success, but I knew it would be folly to pursue a similar approach on my second visit. They'd merely assume I was trying to be clever, so this time I chose a much simpler course of action. It was based on the concept of a blank canvas. Rather than spending hours selecting records according to some vague criterion of "perceptivity", I would pick them at random from my collection. The other members of the society could then make of them what they wished. So it transpired that the following evening I arrived with copies of "All My Ghosts", "Death of a Clown" and "Hurry Up Harry".

George nodded at me gloomily as I traipsed inside.

"Number four," he declared. "Better than an empty house, I suppose."

I bought a pint of Guinness, then went through to the back room. Seated around the table were Chris, Keith and Mike.

"Aha," said Chris, when he saw me. "The secret envoy."

"We thought you had a genuine interest," Keith added, "but you were just spying on us."

Presumably Mike had given the game away. He did look slightly guilty.

"I'm not a spy," I said. "I'm trying to improve relations."

"You've got a funny way of going about it," Chris remarked.

"Well," I said, glancing at Mike, "at least I'm not a turncoat."

In spite of the cool reception it seemed they had no intention of ejecting me. I was unsure whether this was because they were more liberal than the Forensic Records Society, or simply because they wanted to make up the numbers. Whatever the motive, they offered me a seat and Chris quickly got the meeting underway.

"Alright, Mike," he said. "Would you like to begin?"

Mike's presence was yet to be explained, but when he revealed his first record I began to get an inkling. He'd chosen "No Particular Place to Go".

"Two minutes forty-two seconds," he announced. "Can I say something before we play it?"

"Certainly," said Chris.

"It's only a minor point."

"Doesn't matter."

"Right."

Mike paused for a second or two while he composed himself.

"The pitch of the guitar," he said, "reminds me of an angry Yellow Cab in heavy traffic."

"Must be to do with the tuning," said Keith.

"Yes."

"Been to New York, have you?" Chris asked.

"Went there on a pilgrimage," Mike replied. "Nearly got run over."

That was all he wanted to say, so Keith started the record and we sat listening closely. After it finished there was a long silence; then Chris quoted the line about the safety belt that didn't budge. It was a poignant moment, and we could all imagine the way he felt. Furthermore, we were aware that neither Mike's comment nor Chris's quotation would have been allowed under James's rigorous auspices. (Judgement, in this case, was quite unnecessary.) With these sobering thoughts in mind we continued the session, and for his opening choice Chris produced a copy of "Just Passing".

"If this was a portrait," he said, "it would be classified as a miniature."

The running time wasn't shown on the label, but I guessed it was barely more than a minute in length. Mike had evidently never heard it before: he sat gazing transfixed at the record as it whirled round and round on the turntable. Chris and Keith were similarly enthralled, and during that short period I realised that none of them were guilty of disloyalty. Regardless of their protestations they were all ingrained forensic men. The only difference was that they were now known by another name. However, I had no idea if this made my task easier or more difficult.

During the next hour or so we listened to several interesting recordings (including "Hurry Up Harry", which caused Chris to raise his eyebrows); then, as the evening drew to a close, Keith submitted a long-player. The song he'd chosen was "Time Has Told Me". This provided a perfect opening.

"So," I said, after it had ended, "has time told you yet?"

"Told me what?" Keith enquired.

"You said time would tell," I explained, "when I asked you about coming back on Mondays."

"Oh yes," he said. "I did, didn't I?"

"I was just wondering if you'd reached a decision."

"Well . . ."

"Hang on a sec," said Mike. "I thought we were supposed to be sharing our perceptions."

"We are," Keith replied.

"Doesn't sound like it."

"Sorry," I said. "My fault."

Mike was most indignant about the way we'd casually drifted off the beaten track, but Chris intervened swiftly to smooth his ruffled feathers.

"We share our perceptions," he affirmed, "simply by playing records to one another."

"You mean we don't need to analyse them in depth?" enquired Mike.

"Not unless you want to," said Chris. "You can if you like."

"No, no, it's alright."

The long-player was lying motionless on the deck, and Mike spent a while peering studiously at the label.

"*Five Leaves Left*," he murmured, as if committing the words to memory. "Five. Leaves. Left."

Once again Chris raised his eyebrows. It seemed that the Perceptive Records Society had made a significant conquest, and I was at a complete loss as to what my next move should be.

136

"That's one of the problems with Mondays," remarked Keith. "Long-players aren't allowed."

"True," I said. "I'll concede that."

"Next Wednesday, for example, I was thinking of bringing the long version of 'Voodoo Chile'."

"Oh yes?"

"But on a Monday it would be strictly forbidden."

During this brief exchange Mike had sat gazing vaguely across the table. Now, however, he suddenly snapped out of his reverie.

" 'Voodoo Chile'!" he intoned. "Five minutes eleven seconds!"

Keith shook his head.

"No," he said. "You're thinking of 'Slight Return'."

"How do you mean?"

"The short version is subtitled 'Slight Return'," Keith replied, "but there's also a long version with different musicians."

"Blimey," said Mike. "I never knew."

Needless to say there was no question whether Mike would be coming back the following Wednesday, if only out of sheer curiosity. The look on his face suggested a whole new world was opening up before him. Meantime, the future of the Forensic Records Society remained unclear.

Looming large in the background was the menace posed by Phillip and his swarm of admirers. From the moment I awoke on Thursday morning I felt apprehensive about the forthcoming meeting in the Public Hall. To judge from recent developments, the CRS was rapidly evolving into a formidable organisation whose reach extended further each day. To make matters worse, I gradually became aware of some kind of magnetic force that was trying to drag me towards its centre. At first it was barely noticeable, but by the early evening I found myself being drawn irresistibly in the direction of the Meeting Hall. Fortunately I had enough self-possession to regard the situation objectively, as though I was taking part in a scientific exercise. It was the others I felt sorry for: the unsuspecting majority who had no inkling they were being controlled and exploited. When I arrived at eight o'clock there were already hordes of people heading through the gateway, many of them carrying small square boxes with neat handles on their lids. It was a warm spring evening and they were being greeted at the top of the steps by the two Andrews, both wearing sunglasses and sporting flowery ties. Spaced at regular intervals along each side of the hall were large posters of Phillip, smiling benignly and inviting all and sundry to come and confess. I paused outside the railings, resolute in my determination to proceed no further, and suddenly I spotted Mike standing a short distance away. He was peering with interest at the advancing crowds, but I could tell at a glance that, like me, he had no intention of going inside. I walked over and joined him.

"Come to see what all the fuss is about?" I asked.

He was fully preoccupied and my words made him jump.

"Oh hello," he said, once he'd recovered himself. "Yes, I thought I might have a look."

"It's like lambs to the slaughter."

"Yep."

Just then, from within the Meeting Hall, came the sound of a record being played. I recognised the song straightaway, and as a sorrowful voice began warbling I couldn't help but smile to myself. Mike, however, had plainly never heard it before. He stood listening closely with a baffled expression on his face.

"What's he talking about?" he demanded at length. "What's all this about leaving a cake out in the rain?"

"Don't ask me," I replied. "It's one of the great unsolved mysteries."

We resumed our vigil as the ballad wended its tortuous way towards its climax. By this time the hall was almost full and the flow of prospective confessors had diminished to a trickle. In consequence, Mike and I were fairly conspicuous as we loitered outside the railings. It was obvious the two Andrews would have noticed us, and when finally they slipped inside I had no doubt they'd report our presence to Phillip immediately. Even so, my duty as a neutral observer obliged me to stay just a little bit longer. I was unsure what course a mass confession might take exactly, and for the present I could only guess what was going on behind the closed doors.

After the record finished there was a loud "clunk" as a public address system was plugged in; then a few seconds later we heard words being spoken in a rich, resonant tone. The voice belonged unmistakably to Phillip, but for some reason he was employing a slight American accent.

"Good evening," he began. "I bid you welcome. Welcome to those who witnessed the birth of our humble society, and those who joined us as we took our first steps into the wider world. Since then we've achieved much and we still have much to achieve."

He continued in this manner for several minutes, during which he was accompanied by assorted cheers, screams and whoops from his audience. Ultimately, though, he got down to business.

"Alright," he said. "Now have we brought all our yesterdays? . . . I'm sorry . . . my apologies . . . have we all brought our yesterdays?"

Another cheer signalled that the answer was yes.

"Good," said Phillip. "Very good." His voice softened as he held the microphone closer to his lips. "Now I want you to come down to the front, one by one, and confess to me in person."

There was a prolonged shuffling of feet, then all at once an eerie silence descended over the Meeting Hall. Even the surrounding streets seemed to go quiet in anticipation of what was to follow. Once or twice during the next half-hour I thought I heard the desultory rise and fall of a string quartet, somewhere deep in the heart of the building, but it was too faint to be certain. Mike and I stood together gazing through the railings, listening to nothing in particular, both of us awestruck by the immensity of the occasion.

After a while the door opened and the two Andrews emerged, carefully closing it behind them. From this distance they appeared to have a surreptitious air about them, so I watched them closely as they paused at the top of the steps and glanced all around.

"I think they're looking for us," said Mike.

"And they've spotted us too," I replied. "Here they come."

Even as I spoke the pair of them nodded to one another, then moved swiftly down the steps.

"Let's go," I said. "We don't want to get involved with that lot."

We turned on our heels and began walking in the opposite direction.

"Hey!" called a voice behind us. "Wait!"

We sped up, and so did they.

"I wish I hadn't bothered coming," Mike panted. By now we were almost having to run, and our pursuers were still drawing nearer.

"We only want to talk!" cried one of them, but we ignored the plea and kept going. Eventually they gave up.

"That was close," I said, when we were several streets away. "I'm going to steer clear of that place in future."

"Me too," said Mike.

By complete chance we'd ended up outside the Half Moon, so we decided to drop in for a pint. The pub turned out to be fairly busy, and I for one found it quite a relief to be back amongst normal Thursday-evening customers. Mike, though, was having difficulty shrugging off recent memories.

"I can't understand it," he said, as we settled down at our usual corner table. "Why would somebody bake a cake and then leave it out in the rain?"

"Probably a metaphor," I ventured. "You know, like Mrs Robinson and her cup cakes."

Mike peered at me uncomprehendingly.

"Sorry," he said. "You've lost me entirely now."

Privately it occurred to me that Mike ought to take his enquiries to the Perceptive Records Society. Let them try and explain the meaning of everything. I realised, however, that it would be churlish to voice my inner thoughts. Instead I changed the subject to more pressing matters.

"How long," I said, "before Phillip hires a football stadium to hold his meetings?"

"Good question," Mike replied.

"The way he takes advantage of his people is most alarming."

"Yes, but it's their choice, isn't it?"

"How do you mean?"

"Well," said Mike, "they go to the meetings of their own accord so they must know what they're letting themselves in for."

"Suppose so."

"If they want to be fleeced for a fiver every week it's up to them," he added. "It makes no difference to us."

"'Us' being who?" I asked.

"The forensics, of course," he said, with disbelief. "Who do you think I mean?"

"Oh," I said. "So you're not abandoning the cause then?"

"Of course not!"

"But you spent last night with the perceptives."

"All part of the same movement as far as I'm concerned," said Mike. "They're just an offshoot."

It was gratifying to hear him talk like this, and I began to get a clearer picture of his allegiances. Nevertheless he proceeded to make it plain that he was dissatisfied with the current arrangements and would probably give the Monday session a miss for a week or two.

"James is too strict," he said bluntly. "At least Chris and Keith give me a bit of freedom."

"What about the CRS?" I asked. "I presume you don't count them as part of the same movement."

"No," said Mike. "They're not serious about music."

"They play good records now and again."

"Maybe they do," he said, "but only by accident."

It was my turn to buy a round of drinks, so I went over to the bar and quickly got served by George. He was in a relatively good mood.

"Some friends of yours were here last night," he said, indicating the wall opposite. I followed his gaze and saw that another notice had recently appeared:

NEW FORENSIC RECORDS SOCIETY
MEETS HERE
TUESDAYS 9PM
BRING THREE RECORDS OF YOUR CHOICE

I read the words with astonishment, then read them again just to make sure I wasn't mistaken, but there was no doubt about it. The implications were shattering. The upstart society was patently much more than a mere "offshoot" (to use Mike's expression). On the contrary, all the evidence signalled that we were in the midst of a coup. The culprits had pounced on the vacant Tuesday-night slot with the obvious aim of stepping directly into our shoes. Furthermore, they had lots of time on their side. It was only Thursday, which gave them the best part of a week to organise a recruitment drive. For a brief instant I felt impelled to rush round and tell James the disastrous news, and perhaps even urge him to take countermeasures. In the back of my mind, however, I knew such efforts would be futile. After all, it was James's intractability that lay at the root of all the disaffection we'd experienced. He was hardly going to change his ways at this late stage, so I was left with a stark choice between deserting him or remaining loyal. It goes without saying I chose the latter course.

George was naturally elated at the prospect of some extra business. He was whistling a merry tune as he filled our glasses and placed them on the counter.

"So who put the notice up?" I enquired.

"I just told you," George replied. "Some friends of yours."

"Yes, but who exactly?"

"Can't say any more," he announced. "It's a commercial agreement."

Despite his obfuscation George actually told me quite a lot. I'd already guessed who the suspects were, and I now knew they were paying for the privilege of hiring the back room. This in turn meant they were deadly serious in their intentions. All of a sudden I recalled the evening when Dave, Barry and Rupert had spoken to one another in urgent whispers. In retrospect I saw clearly how these murmurings had spawned a conspiracy, and I couldn't avoid a sense of despair at their foolhardiness. Here we were facing the threat of annihilation by the CRS, and they'd chosen this very moment to undermine our leadership! I assumed their objective was to recast the Forensic Records Society in a mould of their own devising (hence the prefix "New"). Yet the original guidelines laid down by James had proved indispensable time and again. True enough, he tended to be rather severe in their enforcement, but I doubted if the challengers would ever find a better system. Indeed, once they'd seized the helm they were likely to be just as restrictive as him.

I was still pondering this state of affairs when I became aware of excited voices coming from the street outside. It sounded as if a great multitude was approaching the Half Moon, and seconds later the double doors swung open. I watched in dismay as the pub was gradually swamped with men and women clad in T-shirts bearing the words: I CONFESSED. Seemingly the Confessional Records Society had decided to adopt the place for their socialising. It was a free country, of course, and this was their prerogative. All the same, I had no wish to be overrun by a crowd of babbling zealots. It was a shame really. In appearance and conduct they were barely different to forensic people (as a matter of fact, from my observations they were unfailingly friendly, generous and considerate to others). For reasons of their own, however, they regarded records in a completely different light to us. They viewed them as little more than props and accessories, and saw no intrinsic value in the records themselves. Accordingly there existed a gulf between the two persuasions which could never be bridged.

I was highly tempted to make a swift exit, especially when it occurred to me that Phillip and the two Andrews might turn up at any minute. The reality, though, was that I'd just purchased two pints of beer. Nobody was leaving until they'd been drunk. I made my way through the throng and rejoined Mike, who was eyeing the newcomers warily.

"Hard to imagine now," he said, "but it's only a couple of weeks since I attended a confession myself."

"Oh yes," I replied. "I'd forgotten about that."

"Luckily they rejected me."

"Yes."

There was a slight possibility that we might be recognised, but actually the confessionals were so wrapped up in their own world they remained blissfully unaware of us. As a consequence we were able to eavesdrop without being detected. We listened in fascination while they relived their precious few seconds alone with Phillip (apparently they had to queue for this); and we quickly learnt that he'd already taken advance payment for future engagements. We also discovered the name of the record he'd chosen for the next mass confession: "My Heart Will Go On".

"We could do with one or two icebergs around here," Mike remarked. "It's getting a bit hot and sticky."

"Do you want to get going then?" I asked.

"Yeah."

We finished our pints and headed for the door. Outside, darkness had fallen. Mike and I said goodnight and we went our separate ways, and only after he'd gone did I realise I'd neglected to tell him about the New Forensic Records Society. Too late now. Perhaps he'd find out for himself in the coming days; or maybe he already knew but had avoided the subject to spare my feelings. Either way, it scarcely made any difference. The unvarnished truth was that there were now three separate record societies each with the same basic purpose.

When I got home I went straight to my turntable and played "Substitute" three times in succession. After that there was nothing I could do except wait patiently for Monday to come around.

Fortunately I had plenty to occupy me. Following my last visit to James's house I'd decided to embark on a side-project of my own. My plan was to play all my records that faded in *and* out. In the event it took me longer to find them than to play them. After hours of research I came up with "Ambassador of Love", "I Wanna Be Adored", "Boys Better", "I See the Light", "Geno" and "Here We Go Round the Mulberry Bush".

The latter title was turning out to be something of a perennial, and while it was playing I considered the short history of the Forensic Records Society. Back in the winter we'd started out with such high ideals that the difficulties we now faced would have been almost inconceivable. Yet within a few months we'd witnessed bickering, desertion, subterfuge and rivalry. I was rapidly coming to the conclusion that only a miracle could save us now.

At eight o'clock on Monday evening I arrived at the Half Moon and found that Alice had exchanged duties with George. I had no idea if this was temporary or permanent, but for the time being she was running the main bar while he oversaw operations in the back room. Vaguely I recalled a similar swap taking place on a previous occasion, and as I went through to join James I wondered what the reason could be.

Unsurprisingly there were no other members present, but in spite of this James seemed wholly unconcerned. He sat presiding over the red portable as though it was a normal Monday session. George, however, was hovering restlessly behind the corner bar, plainly apprehensive about his dwindling sales. As a gesture of goodwill, therefore, I immediately went and bought a pint apiece for me and James.

"Rather quiet," I said, when I took my place opposite him.

"Can't be helped," James replied.

"Shall we wait another five minutes, just in case?"

"No," he said. "We can't change our policy because of other people's failures." He went over to the door and closed it firmly. "Latecomers will not be admitted," he announced. "Now, would you like to begin?"

In view of such a sparse turnout I'd been expecting the meeting to be awkward and embarrassing, but actually James's insistence on maintaining the formalities made it much easier. All we had to do was take turns and submit our records. The fact that we weren't allowed comments, judgements or quotations made the procedure beautifully simple.

My opening selection was "I'm Your Puppet", and James responded with "Games People Play". I then chose "If I Were a Carpenter", James followed with "Reason to Believe", and while we were listening the thought struck me that all these recordings were roughly of the same ilk. Generally our Monday gatherings were characterised by a huge variety of styles and performances, yet tonight we appeared to have stumbled into one particular field. Moreover my next choice was "Morning Dew", a song which again fell into the same broad category. I spent several moments debating whether this could have any significance, but ultimately I decided it was probably nothing more than chance.

In the meantime James went to the corner bar and bought another couple of pints. As I awaited his return my eyes gradually strayed across the table to where his final record was lying. With a sudden jolt I noticed its plain white label, completely blank except for some figures handwritten in ink, and I realised that once again I was looking at Alice's demo.

I swiftly averted my gaze when James rejoined me carrying two full glasses. He placed them between us and sat down; then he slipped the record from its sleeve and put it on the deck. At this point I sensed that James wished to say something, but being constrained by his own rules he was obliged to remain silent. Instead, we passed a minute or so watching the froth on our beers settle. In the background I was aware that George had run out of jobs to do and was now peering at us curiously from behind his counter.

"Anything wrong?" he enquired at length.

"No, no," James replied; and at last he reached over and switched the record on. The sound that emerged from the red portable was at once serene, solemn and mesmerising: a guitar blending perfectly with a voice; the words insightful; the melody sweet yet subdued.

After it ended we said nothing. This was not because of our doctrine but because really there was nothing left to say. We'd listened to it forensically and that was all we could do.

James offered no explanation as to why Alice had relented about her record being played to other people (especially me). He merely lifted it from the turntable and returned it to its sleeve.

George, of course, was subject to none of our conventions, yet he too was seemingly lost for words. Throughout the rendition he stood statuesque at his post as if a spell had been cast upon him. Even when it finished he didn't move for a good while; and I saw that his eyes were glistening, perhaps with some distant memory of times long gone.

The session was now officially over, so James unplugged the red portable and began packing it away. I collected my three records together, nodded at George, and then carried my pint through to the main bar. The clock told me it was half past ten, although I couldn't imagine where the time had gone. Alice was busy serving some customers, but I saw her glance in my direction as I headed for our usual corner table. As soon as she was free she vanished into the back room, and shortly afterwards George came out and resumed his former duties. He looked thoroughly bewildered by the ceaseless swaps and changes.

I didn't see Alice again that evening, but eventually James appeared bearing in his arms the red portable. I went and held open the cellar door, and he descended the steps. A few minutes later he joined me at the table.

He was still in a sombre mood, and for a long period we both sat there quietly reflecting on our situation. The outlook was mixed to say the least. On the positive side, we'd finally had a public airing of Alice's demo. Set against this, though, was the pronounced absence of all the other members of the Forensic Records Society. Something plainly needed to be done, but I was mildly surprised when I heard James's solution.

"Well," he said, abruptly ending the silence, "if they won't come to us, we'll just have to go to them."

"What?" I demanded. "You mean the New Forensics?"

"Yes."

"But I thought you of all people would never surrender."

"It's not a matter of surrendering," said James, "but I'm afraid we have no choice but to grasp the nettle."

His proposition was to attend the opening meeting of the New Forensic Records Society, and to ask some awkward questions.

"We'll get them to outline their founding precepts," he explained. "Most likely they won't have given them any proper consideration, and with any luck we'll make them see the errors of their ways."

For my part I considered the plan to be highly risky, but James insisted we could carry it off. Accordingly we agreed to visit the Half Moon the following evening, and to ensure we arrived together we arranged to rendezvous outside.

When I got home I went straight to my turntable and played "Eve of Destruction" three times in succession; then I lay on my bed and reviewed our prospects.

The problem with James's strategy was that it assumed the New Forensic Records Society comprised a bunch of novices, whereas actually they were seasoned veterans of the forensic process. Dave, Barry and Rupert were perfectly capable of contriving their own set of precepts, and for all we knew they may have come up with a superior formula. After all, they'd seen for themselves the limitations of allowing no comments, judgements or quotations. Perhaps they'd even gone so far as to abolish these regulations altogether. Barry seemed especially well versed in constitutional issues and I could easily envisage him putting pen to paper when it came to drawing up the rules.

Furthermore, I'd long suspected him of harbouring ambitions of his own. He clearly envied James and it was quite possible that the new society had been established simply to give him the power he craved.

I spent the next day carefully selecting my three records for the inaugural session; then when evening came I headed for the Half Moon. James was waiting outside as arranged.

"Ready and willing?" he enquired.

"Yep."

"Right," he said. "Let me do the talking."

When we got inside we saw that a minor incident was taking place. George was standing at the top of the cellar stairs, barring the way to Barry who was trying his best to get past.

"I've told you twice," said George. "You can't go down there."

"But I need to get the red portable," Barry protested. "The meeting starts in five minutes."

He evidently assumed the red portable belonged to the Forensic Records Society; and that he was therefore free to appropriate it for his own purposes. George, however, was immovable.

"Sorry," he said. "You'll have to get permission from the owner."

While this conversation was going on I'd noticed there were several newcomers in the pub. They were all watching the exchange with interest, and I guessed most of them were recruits for the New Forensic Records Society.

Barry was standing with his back to us, but now in exasperation he turned away from George and found himself face-to-face with me and James.

"Oh," he said, plainly startled. "You've come to join us, have you?"

"Yes," James replied. "Something amiss?"

"He wants to use your record player," announced George. "I've told him he'll have to ask you."

At these words Barry stiffened visibly.

"It's yours, is it?" he said.

"I'm afraid so," James answered.

"I see."

Barry was unable to hide his dismay at the revelation, and I realised that James had the opportunity to smother the new society at birth merely by denying access to the red portable. Instead, though, he pulled a veritable masterstroke.

"Would you like to borrow it?" he asked.

"You mean you don't mind?" said Barry.

"Not if it's in a good cause, no."

"Well, we are a forensic society."

"That's alright then."

"Thanks very much," said Barry. "Very generous of you."

He continued to bow and scrape for a little longer, then headed down into the cellar to fetch the red portable. I glanced briefly at James but he showed no sign of having triumphed. Nonetheless the past few moments had seen a crisis forestalled. Barry's supplication had been witnessed by numerous onlookers (including Dave and Rupert) and I knew for sure that James had regained the advantage.

When we went through to the back room I discovered that the corner bar was not in use. There was no sign of Alice and I supposed she had other commitments for the evening. A second discovery was rather less obvious, but gradually I discerned that the so-called recruits were actually friends of Barry and Dave. They included some women, a fact which represented a positive step for the forensic movement in general. Even so, it swiftly became clear that the meeting had been "packed" in order to give it the veneer of success. First of all I noticed the nods of recognition the newcomers gave one another as they took their seats around the table; and it later struck me that none of them were being particularly attentive when the records were playing (I even saw somebody stifling a yawn). Fortunately I could tell that James was equally aware of the deception; and no doubt he would adjust his tactics accordingly.

Despite the slight delay the session proceeded more or less on schedule. Barry presided over the red portable and we heard a number of engaging contributions, such as "Heart Don't Leap" and "The Beginning of the Twist". At the conclusion of each record Dave enquired whether there were any comments or judgements. Initially there were none, but as the evening unfolded the situation started slowly to change. My opening choice was "Shipbuilding", and when it finished there was the usual prolonged silence. After a polite pause Dave spoke.

"OK," he said. "Are there any comments or judgements?"

"Well, it's alright to listen to," remarked the woman sitting opposite me, "but you can't really dance to it, can you?"

Nothing else was said, and so we moved on.

Barry had brought "Driving Away From Home", and Rupert followed with "Everything I Own". Neither of these produced any comments or judgements, and then it was James's turn. To my astonishment he handed

Barry a record with a plain white label, completely blank except for some figures handwritten in ink. The idea had never occurred to me that James would present Alice's demo in a rival session, yet here it was lying before us. Presumably the gambit was all part of his grand scheme. I felt a stir of expectation pass around the table as Barry placed the record on the deck and switched on. This was only the second time I'd heard it, and again the sound that emerged from the red portable was at once serene, solemn and mesmerising: the guitar blending perfectly with the voice; the words insightful; the melody sweet yet subdued.

While it was playing I thought I detected a draught in the room, fromsomewhere behind me. It was barely perceptible, and I guessed that a latecomer had stealthily opened the door and come inside. Nobody else appeared to notice. Everyone was gazing transfixed at the turntable when the record reached its end and stopped. There was a long silence, which was finally broken by Dave.

"OK," he said. "Are there any comments or judgements?"

"Well, it's alright," remarked the woman sitting opposite me, "but you can't really dance to it, can you?"

"What!?" cried an irate voice behind me.

Everybody looked up in alarm as Alice marched across the room, seized the record from the deck and smashed it over James's head.

"There!" she snapped. "You can't dance to it now, can you?"

Next instant she turned and went stalking out of the room, slamming the door behind her.

Another stir passed around the table.

"Any more comments or judgements?" asked Dave.

He'd evidently decided that the best course of action was to continue the meeting as though nothing had happened.

"Not that I can think of," said James.

The record had broken into two halves, and as I watched him gather up the pieces it struck me that he might have overplayed his hand. This was a shame really because when the evening began the odds had been stacked in his favour. His reputation for integrity, alongside his ownership of the red portable, had bestowed on him a degree of authority in the eyes of all present. Now, however, he'd suffered public humiliation; and he was hardly in a position to question Dave and Barry about their founding precepts. The intention of our visit was to demonstrate the errors of their ways, but it seemed the plan would now have to be discarded.

Nevertheless, as the session resumed I started to sense that a lesson had been learned. The next record we heard was "Ain't That Enough", and when it finished Dave declined to ask if there were any comments or judgements. It was the same for the next record, and the one after that. In fact, by the end of the meeting it was patently clear that the practice had been abandoned. Barry merely played the records and returned them to their sleeves. I glanced at him once or twice and thought he looked rather despondent. Perhaps he'd realised there was nothing new about the

New Forensic Records Society; and that his bid for independence had been entirely fruitless.

Certainly he showed scant gratitude when he restored the red portable to its rightful owner. Without ceremony he handed it to James and muttered a curt "thank you" before heading out to the main bar with his companions. For a few moments James and I were alone, but I decided not to mention Alice's abrupt departure. Instead I broached the subject of the Perceptive Records Society. They were due to meet the following evening.

"Do you want me to continue my diplomatic mission?" I enquired. "I know you're quite sceptical about it."

"Well, I was at the outset," James replied, "but lately I've come to the conclusion that maybe a little compromise is called for."

"Really?"

"It'll do no harm to keep all channels open."

"Oh," I said. "Will you be joining me then?"

"No," said James. "You're doing perfectly alright on your own."

With this endorsement ringing in my ears I emerged from the back room and discovered it was five past eleven. All but a few people had departed. Normally at this hour George would be busy closing the bar and brusquely ordering dawdlers to leave the premises. Tonight, though, he was in an altogether different mood. He could almost be described as mellow. He stood behind his counter slowly polishing a glass, and when I passed by I noticed his eyes were glistening.

"Goodnight, George," I said.

"Goodnight," he answered, but plainly his mind was far away.

When I got home I went straight to my turntable and played "Mentally Murdered" three times in succession; then I lay on my bed and dozed fitfully. To tell the truth I was exhausted. In less than twenty-four hours I was destined to attend a meeting of the Perceptive Records Society. It would be my third consecutive foray in a week and I was beginning to feel as if I was on some sort of treadmill, yet it was unthinkable to cry off at this crucial stage. I knew I had no choice except to ride the wave and see where it took me.

Thankfully the perceptives weren't considered to be a "hostile" party. On the contrary, I found them very welcoming when I arrived at the Half Moon the next evening. There was even a space reserved for me at the round table: a near-perfect position equidistant between the quadrophonic speakers. All the same, I sensed I was under close scrutiny once the session began. Chris, Barry and Mike were well aware of my forensic leanings and by now they must have been wondering why I kept coming back week after week. For my part I had no wish to arouse their suspicions unnecessarily, but I was equally determined not to share my perceptions with anybody. In consequence my first selection was "MMM MMM MMM MMM", a record which I regarded as wholly impenetrable.

Keith responded rather predictably with "21st Century Schizoid Man"; Mike followed with "Spock's Missing"; and Chris completed the opening set with "Somewhere Across Forever".

So far, so perceptive.

Undoubtedly these were all excellent choices, yet I couldn't help thinking my hosts were keeping their big guns in reserve. My intuition told me to prepare for a surprise: some masterful recording that would force me to bow to their supremacy. Meanwhile I continued to act as though it was business as usual.

My next presentation was "Time Has Come Today", to which they all listened attentively, and then Keith revealed his second offering. It was a record with a plain white label, entirely blank except for the figures 9/25 handwritten in ink.

"Where did you get that?" I asked with amazement.

"I'm afraid I can't tell you," said Keith, "but, believe me, I had to jump through a lot of hoops."

He placed it on the deck and lowered the arm. The sound that emerged from the speakers was at once serene, solemn and mesmerising: the guitar blending perfectly with the voice; the words insightful; the melody sweet yet subdued.

I glanced around the table and noticed Mike was holding a stopwatch.

"Blimey," he said, when the record ended. "Three minutes precisely."

"Perfect," remarked Chris.

In the same instant the door opened and George burst into the room. His eyes were gleaming fiercely.

"Whose record is that?" he demanded.

"Mine," Keith replied, removing it from the deck and returning it to its sleeve.

"How much do you want for it?"

By now George had crossed the floor and was standing over us.

"Sorry," said Keith. "It's not for sale."

Chris, Mike and I gazed at one another in silence. We all understood why Keith was unwilling to part with his trophy. George, however, refused to take no for an answer. He reached into his trouser pocket and withdrew a large bundle of banknotes.

"How about twenty?" he said, peeling off the amount and holding it in his other hand.

"No thanks," said Keith. "It's extremely rare and I obtained it only with great difficulty."

"Forty," said George. He peeled off a second note.

"Sorry."

"Sixty."

I'd never seen George behaving like this before. On all questions of money he was normally best described as highly acquisitive, but tonight he'd gone completely out of character. I could only assume his desire to possess the record had got the better of him.

In the meantime Keith was struggling to resist the pressure.

"Why don't I make a few enquiries," he suggested, "and see if I can get you a copy?"

"I thought you said it was rare," George retorted.

"Well, yes . . . it is."

"Hardly worth the effort then."

"But . . ."

"Look," said George flatly, "you might as well sell it to me while you've got the chance. Name your price and let's be done with all this shilly-shallying."

Sad to say, Keith failed the ultimate test.

Chris, Mike and I watched with consternation as eventually he buckled under George's ceaseless onslaught, accepted a sum which I will not disclose, and handed over the record.

"Good lad," said George. "I'll leave you a pint in the pump for luck."

Keith waited until his tormentor had departed, then turned to the rest of us and apologised for his weakness.

"Can't be helped," said Chris. "Forget it."

I remember little about the remainder of the session. No doubt we played several more records and greeted them with keen ears, but in truth the memory is dim. All I know for certain is that the four of us agreed to steer well clear of the Public Meeting Hall on Thursday evening. The episode with George had exposed the vulnerability of the Perceptive Records Society, and the last thing any of us needed was a brush with the confessionals.

As it transpired, though, they had serious problems of their own. During the next day or two I heard reports that the Thursday meeting had dissolved into a debacle, with several people fainting amid displays of mass hysteria. I considered myself fortunate to have avoided these excesses.

A secondary development came in the form of an invitation. It arrived by post on Friday morning and read as follows:

YOU ARE CORDIALLY INVITED TO ATTEND
"A GRAND UNVEILING"
AT
THE HALF MOON
MONDAY 7PM

The envelope was addressed to me care of the Forensic Records Group. I later discovered that James, Chris, Mike, Dave, Barry, Rupert and Keith had all received identical invitations. It seemed George was oblivious to the divisions that lay between the various societies, and saw us merely as members of a composite "group".

There was no hint as to what exactly was being grandly unveiled. Accordingly, we were a curious bunch when we arrived at seven on Monday evening. The only clue was a small glass cabinet which had been mounted high on the wall behind the bar, and which was temporarily hidden by a velvet curtain. The rest of the pub was looking very spick-and-span, and George himself was dressed in his best suit. I was pleased to note that James, Barry and Chris were engaged in an earnest discussion on some matter of mutual interest, their previous enmities apparently forgotten. There were a few other guests as well. Mingling amongst them was the woman from the other night, the one who only liked records you could dance to. Her name was

Sandra, and she told me she was rather excited about the grand unveiling.

"You'll be seeing lots more of me in future," she added. "I'm the replacement barmaid."

"Oh yes?"

"You can call me Sandy."

"Thanks."

Our conversation was interrupted by a call to order from George. Once we'd all fallen silent he announced that he'd recently made a purchase. He had saved for the nation a rare record which was in danger of vanishing into oblivion. Now, thanks to his intervention, it was preserved for evermore, safely locked in a glass cabinet. With tears in his eyes he pulled a cord and swished aside the velvet curtains, and we all applauded a record with a plain white label, entirely blank except for some figures handwritten in ink.

"Aren't you going to play it?" somebody enquired.

"Oh no," George replied. "It's far too precious for that."

Seemingly the exhibit was to be viewed henceforth as a historical document. Nobody opposed George's decision, so there it remained.

After the brief ceremony had concluded the beer began to flow in liberal amounts. One or two newcomers assumed that the drinks were on the house but they soon learned they were wrong: we had to pay for them ourselves. Nonetheless, the evening continued in a relaxed and convivial atmosphere. Just before eight o'clock there was a slight lull in proceedings, and James seized the opportunity to issue an invitation of his own.

164

"Would anyone like to come through to the back room," he said, "and listen to some records?"

The response was unanimous. We quickly took our places at the round table while James went down to the cellar and fetched the red portable. In the meantime Sandy volunteered to operate the corner bar, an offer which George gleefully accepted. Naturally all the forensic regulars had brought their records along, and James had taken the further precaution of providing a few extras for potential new recruits. This turned out to be a wise measure. We were about to begin the session when two forlorn figures appeared in the doorway.

"Watch out," murmured Barry. "Here come Pressed Rat and Warthog."

It was the two Andrews, and they were very polite and apologetic. They explained that they'd recently been trying to make contact with us, but they'd been blocked by Phillip who refused to release them from his clutches. They'd only managed to escape when the taxman caught up with him.

"'Taxman'!" exclaimed Mike. "Two minutes thirty-nine seconds."

"'Aahh Mr Wilson,'" added Chris. "'Aahh Mr Heath.'"

Apparently the CRS was on the verge of collapse.

"You can't build a society on sunglasses and flowery ties," remarked James.

"Well, Phillip thought he could," said the first Andrew, "and he funded it from the collection box."

"He was last seen facing some very awkward questions," said the other Andrew.

We swiftly obtained a couple more seats and the pair were welcomed into the Forensic Records Society. In celebration I went to the bar and bought them a pint apiece. I thought Sandy was quite friendly when she served me, paying me lots of attention, and in consequence I found myself making frequent return visits. At one point she mentioned that I needed reconstructing, or converting, or something along those lines. I can't remember exactly; it had all become a bit of a blur by then. I only knew that it was the best evening we'd had to date, and the prospects looked even better.

Hours later I woke up alone in a strange bed. I had no idea where I was, but in the next room I could hear music. It was rising to a crescendo, and reminded me of a rogue elephant on the rampage. Finally it came to an end, and was followed by some faint American voices:

"Yeah, yeah . . . more, more . . . nice . . . play another song . . . yeah, maybe . . . hey, what's happening later on? . . . what's happening? . . . yeah, beautiful . . . yeah, come on, baby . . . I got it . . . yeah, outasight, man; that was really outasight . . . Ha, ha . . . I'm helpless, man; I can't make it . . . you mean, there's no more drink, man? . . . . .oh, more clothes? . . ."

credits